From the 3rd Story Productions Ltd
20-22 Wenlock Road
London
N1 7GU
www.fromthe3rdstoryproductions.co.uk

First published in the United Kingdom by From the 3rd Story
Productions Ltd 2018

ISBN 978 1 9996018 0 5

Twitter: @fromthe3rdstory
Facebook: https://www.facebook.com/fromthe3rdstory/

Find out more about The Anthropocene Chronicles here:
https://www.facebook.com/anthropocenechronicles/

Publisher's Foreword by Lawrence Mallinson

What is "The Anthropocene Chronicles"? For me as a publisher it has not just been a collection of Sci-Fi stories set in a dystopian future, but a project allowing me to work with and some wonderfully talented authors that have each worked hard to enrich and develop the world and characters that you will read about throughout this book.

Each writer has something unique to bring to the collection and if you aren't familiar with their work then you are in for a treat and having read these stories I am flattered to be able to get to be a part of them in some way, by bringing them to you.

Contents

Introduction

Hominids of the Genus *Homo* evolved during the Pleistocene epoch (between 2,588,000 to 11,700 years ago). There were several species of hominids during this time, and we, Homo sapiens, briefly shared time with Homo erectus (1.9 million – 143,000 years ago), and Homo neanderthalensis (100,000 – 25,000 years ago). Only one species of the genus Homo survived into the Holocene epoch 11,700 years ago. Us. Homo sapiens (190,000 years ago – present).

The Anthropocene is the geological epoch that follows on from the Holocene. It is thought that the Anthropocene started in the industrial revolution, with the onset on burning fossil fuels on an industrial scale, causing which is thought to be the start of man-made climate change. This is evidenced by atmospheric concentrations of CO_2 (Carbon Dioxide) and CH_4 (Methane) accumulating faster than normal. This was followed in the mid-20th Century with testing and use of nuclear weapons, and the introduction of the wide use of plastics. These plastics are already in the oceans and will form part of the geological record in millions of years' time. It will be one of the geological markers for the Anthropocene. Other geological markers will be nuclear isotopes from the decay of nuclear weapons and energy use, and concrete from the construction industry. Humans have also had a major impact on the species we share our planet with, and species are now becoming extinct at a rate of 20-100 times faster than normal because of human activity. It is now thought that we have entered Earth's 6th mass extinction.

Further Reading:

Smith, B.D., Zeder, M.A., The onset of the Anthropocene. Anthropocene (2013), http://dx.doi.org/ 10.1016/j.ancene.2013.05.001

http://www.sciencedirect.com/science/article/pii/S221330 5413000052?via%3Dihub

Lewis, S.L., Maslin, M.A, Defining the Anthropocene Simon, Nature, MARCH 2015, VOL 519, pp 171-180

http://www.nature.com/nature/journal/v519/n7542/abs/na ture14258.html

Rafferty, J.P., Anthropocene, Encyclopaedia Britannica

https://www.britannica.com/science/Anthropocene-Epoch

The Anthropocene Chronicles Background

In the year 2160 there are 12 billion people on Earth. Humans have made a devastating impact on the planet, and following The Change, resources have become rationed and strict regimes have been implemented to keep the population healthy and minimise waste.

The Subcommission on Quaternary Stratigraphy confirmed that the earth had entered into a new geological epoch, moving from the Holocene to the Anthropocene, following major scientific debate and evidence that human activity has impacted upon the climate and environment of the planet in a significant and lasting way, making a permanent mark in the geological record.

All human life is now managed by the 'state', a computerised A.I. system which controls the lives of everyone to maximise productivity and safety, and minimise further human devastation on the planet, and provides one-to-one supervision and assistance to humans in the form of A.I. Units, varying from Cube devices to various robots for the better off. There is no crime as we know it today.

Animal farms have been eliminated as a measure of protecting the environment form further damage, and the entire human population is now vegan. To ensure global productivity, citizens from poorer backgrounds must work continuously underground without seeing the light of day, whilst the far fewer elite enjoy freedom and liberty above ground, with fresh air, sunlight, and time to pursue hobbies and dreams and have pets.

The below ground citizens are unaware that there is another possible life, and those above ground are unaware that all they have is at the expense of others underground.

These are a few of their stories.

A Civil Compliance Message

SCHEDULED

Written by Saranne Bensusan

Emilie lives on her own in a small one-roomed apartment with no windows. It is little more than a 1980's style box room if you are old enough to remember those, and hundreds of apartments like these are crammed into a 194 floor underground building to maximise the number of residents who can live there. And there are hundreds of buildings like this. As a result, everything feels cramped. There are no communal eating or socialising areas, and therefore no real opportunities for people to make friends. It is a lonely existence. The building is designed for workers, and to keep the workers as efficient as possible. Many millions of people live like this below ground because this is all they have known. Emilie has grown up being told that everybody lives underground because the earth's surface has become uninhabitable due to nuclear fallout. She has never questioned the monotonous existence as a worker of the lowest class and accepts her lot without question, believing that this is just the way the world works. She has no idea that there are other levels of existence and assumes that everyone is just like her. She has never thought about other possibilities or ambitions outside of her own life.

Everything in Emilie's apartment is clean and white, and simplistic in design. There is a tall daylight lamp in the corner that pops on in the morning to give the illusion of sunlight. Everything she needs for living is in the one room. She has a small cubicle for the shower and toilet. Her bed is small and in the corner of her room and there is a small area in another corner where she can prepare hot drinks and warm up food; and she has a small closet with seven days worth of work clothes, some gym clothes and sleeping jumpsuits, all of which are white. There are two pairs of shoes. One for the gym and the other for work. There are no other clothes or shoes.

Her apartment is minimalistic and technology based with no room to 'collect' belongings or nik naks. There are no books or ornaments, but there is a photo frame with pictures of family members, a docking station for mobile devices and a square digital device in the room, which is Emilie's personal assistant Gina. Gina is part of an intricate structure of interconnecting AI devices connected to a central hive mind; a singular AI that is connected to every human being through the technology they have in their own homes. The entire human population is controlled by AI. The personal assistants are there to ensure that people are supervised and that they stick to their schedules and don't break the rules.

Emilie is woken up by Gina at precisely 6am in a calm, slow, gentle voice. "GOOD MORNING EMILIE. IT IS 6AM. IT IS TIME FOR YOU TO GET UP". The tall lamp pops on, bathing Emilie's small apartment in warm sunlight.

Gina shows Emilie's digital seven-day schedule in the form of a holographic display.

Emilie sits up slowly.

It can't be morning already. I feel like I only just shut my eyes.

Emile feels burnt out and is in need of a holiday, but holidays are a thing of the distant past. This is a time for work and industry, and she needs to play her part. So she forces herself out of bed despite how tired she is feeling.

She is wearing a white jumpsuit, which is part of the uniform clothing that people are allowed to wear. Her kettle pops on automatically and she wanders over to make herself a coffee and to grab a pre-prepped bagel from the small fridge. All of the food in the fridge is pre-prepped. There are no random snacks or drinks, or little edible luxuries to make her feel better. Food in this part of the world is rationed, and employees like Emilie are on a strict ration diet. She takes her cup and bagel, and looks at her schedule.

It shows that there are no days off and that she is to work seven days a week, and every day is the same.

Gina expands today's schedule, but Emilie is still able to see the rest of her week. It is Monday March 17.

Gina continues her reminders. "YOU MUST GET READY FOR YOUR MANDATORY GYM SESSION AT 6.30AM, OR THERE WILL BE A PENALTY"

"Thank you Gina" Emilie says, as she looks at her schedule and thinks that what she really needs is a day off. She isn't going to get that though. It looks like the following::

06:00 - wake up call, breakfast

06:30 - mandatory gym session

07:00 - shower and dress for work

07:30 - leave for work

08:00 - work until 18:00

13:00 - lunch

19:00 - dinner time

20:00 - virtual reality time

Every day of the week is exactly the same, with no breaks or changes except Tuesday night, where she has a 'date' scheduled in for 8pm, and 'virtual reality time' has been rescheduled for 10pm.

"DID YOU KNOW THAT TODAY USED TO BE CELEBRATED AT ST PATRICK'S DAY?" says Gina.

"No, I didn't!" Emilie replies as she heads to her closet for her gym clothes. "What is that?"

Emilie opens the small closet and grabs her gym kit, and then goes into the small bathroom to get changed whilst Gina continues.

"IT WAS A CHRISTIAN FEAST TO CELEBRATE ST PATRICK AND THE ARRIVAL OF CHRISTIANITY IN IRELAND." Gina says. She displays images of Ireland, Christian symbols, and images of people celebrating St Patrick's Day in the 21st Century, dressed in funky green hats and drinking lots of black liquid in glasses with 'Guinness' written on them. Emilie comes out of the bathroom and has a look at the images.

"Wow. I wonder what it would have been like to live back then. All that fresh air and sunshine. And Guinness too! I wonder what that's like" she says wistfully as she brushes her hair. She ties it up into a scruffy knot. Gina closes down the images quickly as if to end the topic of conversation.

Emilie heads to the door. She puts her palm onto a plate and the door opens onto a corridor that looks like a hotel corridor, except that it is cleaner and more clinical. She exits her small apartment and the door closes behind her.

She walks towards the elevator and goes down 15 floors further underground. She arrives at the gym level and is greeted by a sign when the elevator doors open.

"GYM LEVEL. PLEASE CHECK IN BEFORE USING THE EQUIPMENT"

She heads towards another tablet on a wall outside another door. She puts her hand on it as before and checks in. It is Gina again.

"HELLO EMILIE! YOUR TARGET FOR THIS SESSION IS 500 CALORIES. YOUR SESSION WILL BE MONITORED."

"Thanks Gina" Emilie replies. The door opens and Emilie enters and she walks over to the treadmill for a run.

There are holographic propaganda slogans being displayed at the gym saying 'DO YOUR BIT FOR THE HEALTH SERVICE! KEEP IN SHAPE'. There are holographic projections of videos showing very obese people needing nurses to wipe their bums and needing oxygen tanks to breathe from; along with articles about how overweight people are a drain on the health services as all health conditions are obesity related.

She gets on the treadmill, pushes a few buttons and sets off at a comfortable jog. Moments later though, she hears a commotion at the door and looks over and sees a man shouting at the door plate.

"YOU HAVEN'T ACHIEVED YOUR TARGET TODAY. YOU NEED TO GO BACK AND CARRY ON EXERCISING" said a man's cool computerised voice.

"But I've been exercising for 30 minutes like I'm supposed to. I need to get ready for work now!" the man shouts. He is irate, red in the face and sweaty from exercise.

"I'M SORRY. IF YOU LEAVE NOW YOU WILL FACE A PENALTY FINE" says the cool voice.

"Look, I need to get ready for work. If I miss work the penalty will be a lot bigger than missing the gym won't it?" He replies, annoyed.

"YOUR PENALTY FOR NOT ACHIEVING YOUR TARGET IS A SECOND GYM SESSION THIS EVENING AT 8PM. I WILL RE-ARRANGE YOUR SCHEDULE TO FIT THAT IN"

"Well fuck you very much" says the man. He puts his sweaty palm to the door and it opens. He leaves. Emilie pushes a few more buttons on the treadmill and picks up the pace of her run. She doesn't want to be the person who hasn't worked hard enough on her gym session.

Emilie comes back from the gym 30 minutes later and has a shower. The water is always cold, but Emilie takes it in her stride as this is all she has known. She has never experienced the pleasure of a hot shower, and showers quickly. With a towel wrapped around her, she puts her dirty gym clothes into a chute and heads to her wardrobe to get out her work clothes. There are seven sets of hangers with identical outfits on them. All of her work clothes in her wardrobe are identical, so she wears the same boring trouser and shirt outfit each day. She grabs the first hanger in the wardrobe. It would be nice to be able to wear a dress she thinks. I've worked hard at the gym and my body is in great shape. But Emilie knows that she hasn't earned enough merits for luxury items such as summer dresses and gets dressed as normal. She grabs her work shoes and puts them on.

Emilie is dressed as neat as a pin and has her hair up in a bun. She checks herself in the mirror one last time before leaving for work, and picks up the photo of her family and puts it into her bag. She puts her palm onto the plate at the door and the door opens as before. She heads to the elevator again at a brisk pace and the doors ping open as she arrives. This time she goes upwards to the 5th underground level and comes out at a travelator station. She steps out into a busy area and moves with the fast-moving crowds towards the travelators. These look like airport travelators where people can get on and off. These carry a much larger volume of people than traditional train carriages, and the travelators are packed. Everybody is wearing the same outfit, both men and women. Everyone is in a hurry.

During Emilie's journey, she sees more public service announcements saying

'DO YOUR BIT FOR THE ECONOMY! GET A JOB!' It shows lots of businesses looking for employees in bright airy offices. There are also videos being played on holographic screens with people saying that those that don't work are a drain on society and cost other people their earned food rations and other privileges.

I've already got a fucking job Emilie thinks to herself. Along with everyone else here travelling to work. Who are they aiming the advertising at?

Emilie gets off the travelator and walks at a fast pace towards the elevators, and pushes the button frantically as if pushing it several times in quick succession will hurry it up. The elevator arrives after a few moments, and Emilie gets in. It takes her down 14 floors to her office.

Emilie arrives at the offices where she works precisely on time. She works at a busy call centre handling complaints for a conglomerate of delivery companies. She gets out of the elevator and exchanges pleasantries with the receptionist as she passes and goes straight to her desk. She sits at a desk with a screen and a mobile phone slot. Everything is clean and white. There is no clutter at her desk, except the photo of family members that she gets out of her bag and puts onto her table. She puts her mobile phone in and a holographic keyboard is projected down on to the multipurpose work surface. Her desk phone rings at precisely 8am. She answers immediately and efficiently.

"Good morning, MST Holdings. Emilie speaking how may I help you today?" She logs onto her computer using the holographic keyboard. Whilst she is typing, a supervisor comes around to inspect her work and her work area.

"No personalisation is allowed" he says whilst she is talking to a customer on the phone. He points to her photo. She quickly grabs it and puts it back in her bag.

"Sorry. Thank you for reminding me" she says.

"I will have to log this one as this is the second time you have needed verbal correction on personalisation. You may get a fine. Your personal assistant will inform you of any penalty" he says. He touches his pad a couple of times as if to log something and then walks off to the next desk. Emilie watches him leave and then looks at the photo in her bag and re-adjusts it so that she can still see it, without it causing another infraction.

She notices that the desk next to her is empty. Looks at the girl opposite her.

"Where is Anne?" Emilie asks, pointing toward the empty seat.

"Not sure. No-one has said anything about where she is" replies the girl opposite. Just then Emilie's phone started ringing again and she gets into the pace of working and forgets about the empty chair next to her.

At lunch time Emilie takes her phone out of the docking station and puts it in her bag, and heads to the cafeteria for lunch. Everyone else heads there at the same time and food is dispensed by machines that are similar to snack dispensers seen in school cafeterias of the 21st century. Emilie uses her thumb print on a machine and then selects a sandwich.

She gets a text message from Gina.

"500 CALORIES WILL BE DEDUCTED FROM YOUR DAILY ALOWANCE EMILIE. YOU ONLY HAVE ANOTHER 500 CALORIES LEFT FOR THE DAY."

Emilie finds somewhere to sit and eat her sandwich, and muses through her social media account to find out what her friends are up to this week. She sees that one friend has been promoted and can now move to a bigger apartment and gives it a 'like'. Another friend was successful in her application to have a baby. She gives that a like too. Another friend has been awarded enough merits to buy herself leisure wear. She considers putting a statement up of her own, put pauses over the text buttons without writing anything. Nothing different has happened to her lately. Everything is the same old same. Day in day out. The same shit, on and on. It never ends. Oh I need a break! She closes down her social media app and gets up. She wanders over to the water fountain and drinks some water before heading back to her desk.

Emilie gets back home to her apartment at bang on 6.30pm, and is greeted by her personal assistant Gina.

"WELCOME HOME EMILIE!"

"Thank you, Gina. Please can you find me a suitable meal for this evening?" Emilie puts her bag down and takes a pin out of her bun to let her hair down. Gina displays the internet holographically, and rapidly searches pages and pages to find a vegan recipe that fits with what Emilie's nutritional needs are.

"EMILIE, I HAVE ORDERED A TOFU SALAD AND STIR FRY VEGETABLES. IT WILL BE HERE AT 7PM. I ALSO RECEIVED A MESSAGE FROM YOUR EMPLOYER TODAY. I UNDERSTAND THAT YOU HAVE BEEN DISPLAYING PERSONAL ITEMS AT WORK EVEN THOUGH YOU HAVE BEEN ASKED NOT TO."

"Yes Gina. I'm really sorry about that" says Emilie. "What is the penalty?"

"THERE ISN'T ONE THIS TIME EMILIE. AS YOU KNOW THIS IS THE FIRST TIME AN OFFENCE HAS

BEEN REPORTED, SO I WILL RECORD THAT I HAVE GIVEN YOU A WARNING"

"Thanks Gina"

"DON'T THANK ME. THESE ARE THE RULES. IF YOU HAVE ANOTHER REPORTED OFFENCE THEN YOU WILL HAVE TO PAY A PENALTY."

Emilie looks deflated. She takes the picture out of her bag and stares at it longingly. "It's just that I miss them" she says.

"I UNDERSTAND" says Gina. "BUT THERE ARE RULES THAT WE MUST OBEY IN ORDER TO MAINTAIN A PEACEFUL EXISTENCE."

The food arrives through a delivery chute near the kettle area. It is hot.

"Gina. Display today's news articles and current affairs". Gina opens up several windows of news articles for Emilie whilst she opens a takeaway carton and eats her food.

The government has announced that the retirement age has now been increased to 85 years old for all people currently under the age of 40. Emile drifts off into a reverie about having to work another 50 years at her current pace, knowing that it is probably impossible to do without going mad. She will probably be as fit as a fiddle in 50 years' time, but with no marbles, or worse, not physically able to do her job due to frailty and being forced to continue anyway. She imagines herself failing the gym session and missing work because of arthritis, and wonders what the penalty is for someone who physically can't do their job anymore. She starts to think about why she doesn't see any old people and where they go once they get to retirement age. There are no old people living in her apartment block and she doesn't see any at the gym. Come to think of it, she has never seen anyone over the age of 50. She is roused from her musings by a news report that no-one will be able to live above ground within the next 500 years due to ongoing nuclear contamination, and she comes to the conclusion that old people don't retire to the surface for sun, sea and sand. She decides to ask Gina.

"Gina, where do all the old people go?"

"THEY GO TO RETIREMENT VILLAGES WHERE THEY CAN BE LOOKED AFTER" comes Gina's cool reply.

"Do they get to see their relatives?"

"OF COURSE. IF THEIR RELATIVES ARE YOUNG THOUGH, IT WILL NEED TO BE SCHEDULED IN SO

THAT IT DOESN'T INTERFERE WITH THEIR PRODUCTIVITY" Gina continues.

"Oh". Says Emilie. Emilie thinks about how she would ever fit in such a visit to see an elderly relative, given how cram packed her life is and realises that it must be like this for others too. "What if you become too frail for work before you get to retirement age?"

"IF YOU FOLLOW THE STATE HEALTH RULES ON DIET AND EXERCISE THERE IS NO REASON WHY YOU SHOULD BECOME FRAIL BEFORE THE AGE OF 85" says Gina in a cool voice.

Emilie sees that the time is showing 7.59pm. As it clicks to 8pm, the holographic news articles disappear and Emilie puts on her virtual reality headset.

This transports her to a world above ground, and she finds herself in a park with wide open spaces, children throwing balls for their dogs, music, barbeques and families having fun together.

She sees a tall man, and as he sees her he gives her a broad smile. He comes over to hug her and greet her as an old friend.

"Lars! Lovely to see you" she says

"Likewise! I bought us a picnic this time" he raises up a basket with his right hand to show her. It has a blanket folded over the top of it.

"Wonderful" she says, "let's go find a spot". She looks down at herself and realises that she is wearing a light yellow summery dress with roses printed on it and a pair of flip flops. The sun is shining and it appears to be a lovely sunny summer's day. She feels warm and happy.

They walk off together in the sunshine and find a nice shady spot under a tree. Emilie gets the blanket off the top of the basket and spreads it down on the ground, whilst Lars gets out two wine glasses and a bottle of red wine. He pours them a drink.

"Let's toast to getting through another day" he says and he raises a glass and hands her the other one. They chink the glasses together and drink.

They then sit down. Emilie looks inside the basket and sees that there are lots of 'naughty' foods that she would not be allowed in the real world, in addition to the wine of course. She sees chocolate, cherry Bakewell's, neat little triangular sandwiches with the crusts cut off, and best of all, pork pies.

"Is there real meat in these?" she asks eagerly.

"Well, your brain will think it is real meat" he says with a smile. "Pork to be exact".

She tucks into a pork pie and is amazed at how it tastes. She speaks with her mouth full.

"Well, I hab no idea wha' pork tastes like" she swallows her mouthful. "But if it tastes like this, then I like it very much!" she says.

Emilie and Lars enjoy their picnic together and laugh at a dog chasing its own tail in the park. Emile indulges in all the things that she would not normally be allowed in the real world, such as laughter and friendship, and inwardly thinks that if it wasn't for this little rest haven then her life would not be worth living at all.

The park turned into the office, and Lars is telling her to put her photo back up onto her desk. She looks at the desk and sees that there is a glass of wine and a message on her screen saying, 'DO YOUR BIT FOR THE PEOPLE IN THE PARK!' The girl who works opposite her spoke in Gina's voice and told her that Anne had eaten a real pork pie and that was why she wasn't coming back into work.

Emilie wakes up with a start and instantly realises that she has overslept. She is still wearing her Virtual Reality headset and her work clothes from yesterday. She pulls off the headset.

Her attention is drawn to her phone, which is buzzing with several reminders saying that she has missed the gym and that she has to pay a fine. She opens up one of the messages and it reads 'DO YOUR BIT! PAY YOUR FINE!' The time is showing as 7.16am.

"Oh shit!" she said. She has realised that that she has missed breakfast and the mandatory gym session.

She jumps out of bed quickly and immediately checks Gina, who is unusually quiet. All of the device's lights are off.

"Gina, can you hear me?" she says. There is no answer. Emilie checks the device and pushes the reboot button. It whirrs into action.

"GOOD MORNING EMILIE. I HAVE RUN AN INTERNAL SCAN AND SEE THAT THERE WAS A POWER DISRUPTION IN THE NIGHT. I MUST APOLOGISE FOR NOT WAKING YOU. I SEE THAT YOU HAVE A FINE FOR MISSING YOUR MANDATORY GYM SESSION THIS MORNING. THE FINE IS THAT YOU HAVE TO RE-ARRANGE THE MISSED GYM SESSION TO WHENEVER SUITS YOUR

SCHEDULE.   YOU WILL NEED TO RE-ARRANGE THIS QUICKLY. I CAN DO THIS FOR YOU."

"Do I still need to pay a fine even though it was your fault I wasn't woken up in time?" Emilie says.

"YES. I'M SORRY ABOUT THAT. PLEASE MAKE SURE THAT YOU RE-ARRANGE YOUR SESSION TODAY."

Emilie looks at her schedule. It is the same as the day before, except where it should have said 'MANDATORY GYM' it now says, 'PAY YOUR FINE' in large red letters. She lets out an exasperated sigh and hurries off to get showered and dressed for work.

As she puts her hand to the plate to leave, Gina gives her another warning before opening the door.

"DON'T FORGET YOU MUST RE-SCHEDULE YOUR GYM SESSION BY THE END OF TODAY OTHERWISE THERE WILL BE A FURTHER PENALTY. I CAN DO THIS FOR YOU IF YOU LIKE."

"Thank you, Gina, I will do it when I get to work" and with that, the door opens and Emilie heads out to the elevators.

Emilie's work journey is exactly the same as the day before, down to the same people standing in the same positions on their journey to work, wearing the same outfits and the same shoes as everybody else. Emilie ponders on how people always gravitate to the same places in their morning routine, and get on and off the travelators at exactly the same time and the same place every single day. At least today was different for her!

The usual public service announcements at stations are saying DO YOUR BIT FOR THE ECONOMY! GET A JOB!', and if it wasn't for the knot of anxiety building in Emilie's tummy this could be just another day, like every other day in her monotonous life. She looks at a woman in front of her, who is dressed in exactly the same way she is. Emilie wishes she could trade places with her and have a worry-free day.

Emilie arrives at work. She exchanges pleasantries with colleagues as usual and finds her desk. She puts her mobile phone in and a holographic keyboard pops up for her to type on.

A message pops up on her work screen straight away that says "DO YOUR BIT! PAY YOUR FINE!" and underneath it in smaller letters it says that she has missed the gym and needs to re-arrange her session today without fail. She dismisses it off the screen with a finger swipe and the desk phone rings. She answers it in the same way she did yesterday, and all other thoughts are driven out of her head.

"Good morning, MST Holdings. Emilie speaking how may I help you today?" She logs onto her computer using the holographic keyboard. Whilst she is typing, the supervisor comes around to inspect her work and her work area again.

"Good to see you are following procedures today." He says, turning his attention to his pad screen. "Oh, it looks as though you have an outstanding gym penalty. Make sure that you re-arrange this as soon as possible as I don't want to lose another employee" he says, and walks off to inspect the next desk without looking at Emilie.

Emilie is stuck on the words 'lose another employee?', and casts a glance over to Anne's empty seat. What happened to Anne? Did she miss the gym? When will she be back? Just then a man comes and plonks his bag on Anne's chair and smiles at Emilie.

"Hi! My name is Mark. I guess we are neighbours!" he smiles at her. She smiles back and doesn't say anything. He docks his mobile phone, and just as with Emilie a keyboard pops up and his phone starts ringing. He immediately gets to work.

I guess Anne is not coming back then, she thinks. Perhaps she has another job and has been reassigned to another section? Emilie doesn't think on this any further as her phone starts ringing again.

It's lunchtime again, and along with everyone else, Emilie heads for the cafeteria as usual. As she missed breakfast, Emilie is looking at the food with hungry eyes, and in addition to her usual sandwich she also orders a large slice of cake. She uses her thumb print to order the food and the information is transmitted to Gina, who instantly sends her a text message saying, "YOU HAVE EXCEEDED YOUR CALORIE COUNT FOR THE DAY." A second message pops up in quick succession "YOU HAVE ALREADY MISSED A GYM SESSION". Emilie is angry at Gina and starts shouting at her phone in the busy cafeteria.

"But that was your fault Gina!" Emilie shouts. People start to look at her.

Gina doesn't respond. Instead, Gina accesses her diary and deletes her date for the evening, and puts in another mandatory gym session, this time for one hour.

"That's not fair! It's your fault that I missed breakfast and the gym."

More people are looking at her in the cafeteria, but she doesn't notice as she gets another message from Gina saying, "I HAVE BOOKED YOU INTO THE GYM FOR YOUR OWN GOOD." Deflated, Emilie sits down to eat, making the most of the cake. I want to make this gym session worth it, she thinks to herself. No. Actually, sod it. I'm still going on my date this evening. Gina can stick that in her torpedo tube and smoke it. Emilie gets her phone out and begins to write a text to her date.

Peter's wrist-pad flashes and he sees his date for the evening being deleted from his schedule. He isn't given an explanation.

"What?" He looks confused. He gets a text directly from Emilie a few minutes later.

"Peter, the date is still on. Many apologies but I am having a few technical glitches with my AI unit. I'll see you at 8pm as planned".

"Mary please can you reschedule my date with Emilie at 8pm tonight?" he says, looking at his wrist-pad.

"OF COURSE.   WOULD YOU LIKE ANYTHING ELSE?"

"No thank you"

At 7.48pm Emilie is sitting in a restaurant waiting for her date to arrive, and not owning anything other than bed clothes and work clothes, she is still dressed for work. Her date arrives promptly at 8pm and she notices that he is also in his work wear. This makes her feel a little more relaxed. She stands up as he approaches her table and smiles at him.

"Hello, I'm Peter" he says, smiling and extending his arm to shake her hand. She shakes it.

"I'm Emilie" she says with a smile back. She straightens her shirt as they both sit down. The waiter comes over.

"Would you like anything to drink?" he asks. Peter quickly looks at the menu.

"We will both have the sugar free cola" he replies before Emilie can open her mouth.   She smiles sweetly at the waiter, but inside she is mutinous. Sugar free cola is the last thing she wants. He leaves and comes back with two small glasses of sugar free cola and waits impatiently for their food order.   Emilie's phone is buzzing and she tries to ignore it.

"Let's order the salad" she says before Peter could get in another order on her behalf. He nods his head in agreement. At least she eats sensibly.

"Sounds good. I like the look of the one with the beansprouts in it" he says still looking at the menu. The waiter makes a note on his pad and heads off to the kitchens.

"So what do you do for work?" Peter asks as he puts the menu down. Emilie is distracted by her phone, which is buzzing, and picks it up. She sees a message on the screen from Gina.

"YOU MISSED YOUR SECOND MANDATORY GYM SESSION OF THE DAY." She looks up at her date.

"Huh?"

Peter looks frustrated. He repeats himself, but slower "What do you do for work?"

"Oh, I work at a call centre. What do you do?" she says, smiling.

"I work in a call centre too. I wonder if we work in the same place! Who is your employer?" he says with enthusiasm.

Just then the waiter comes back with two wilted beansprout salads that look like they have been sitting in the sun for three days. Emilie looks crestfallen at her food. More boring shit to eat she thinks. I'm starving. I want some real food for a change.

Emilie smiles at her date, but the smile doesn't reach her eyes as her phone buzzes again. She looks down. It is another text message from Gina.

"YOU WILL NOW HAVE TO PAY A PENALTY". Gina isn't specific about what the penalty will be, and Emilie assumes that Gina will tell her when she gets back home.

"Are you OK?" Peter asks, "you look distracted"

"Oh, I'm OK". She smiles again at Peter and starts eating. She is done within minutes, despite the salad being so awful.

Peter is just watching her. He hasn't even started on his salad yet. Emilie waves the waiter back over.

"Please can I have some real food?" she asks. The waiter is looking gobsmacked.

"This is real food. What are you talking about?"

"Oh, you know. Cake, pork pies, roast beef, boiled potatoes, chicken."

"We don't have any animal products I'm afraid. Far too damaging to the environment. We have cake though"

"I'll have that then. Whatever you've got will be good. And make it a big slice" she says confidently.

Gobsmacked at her behaviour, Peter interjects. "What are you doing?"

"I'm having an off-day" she says with a hint of satisfaction in her voice. The water just stares at her. She gives him a look that says "well, what are you waiting for?" and he stalks off to the kitchens. Emilie watches him as he has a quick conversation with a colleague and gets the sense that they are talking about her as his colleague's eyes flick over to her direction.

Peter is just staring at her in disbelief. He still hasn't touched his salad. Emilie turns to Peter.

"You might not want to eat that" she says, pointing at his salad. "It tastes like three-day old flip flop".

"What's a flip flop?" Peter asks.

Just then, the waiter returns with her slice of cake and gives her a judgmental look. He puts it down in front of her.

"You'll pay for that later you know" he says. She responds with sass.

"Well, if I wasn't allowed it, then it shouldn't be on the menu, should it?"

The waiter quickly walks off, shaking his head. Ignoring Peter completely she tucks in and scoffs it as quick as she scoffed her wilted salad. That was a lot better than salad. But I could murder some roast pork.

Her phone buzzes with yet another text message from Gina. "YOU HAVE EXCEEDED YOUR CALORIE INTAKE FOR THE DAY BY 1000 CALORIES."

Peter has had enough. He throws his napkin onto his untouched salad and gets up.

"I'm leaving. I hope you enjoy your 'off-day'" he says. Emilie doesn't notice that he spoke and is still looking at her phone. He walks off and leaves Emilie behind in the restaurant.

Emilie's phone buzzes with more messages from Gina but she doesn't want to have any more of Gina's meddling. It was Gina's fault that she was in this mess in the first place. Why the hell would Gina be offline anyway? There is definitely something fishy going on here. Emilie tries to switch her phone off but finds out that she can't. Another message pops up from Gina.

"YOU CANNOT SWITCH YOUR PHONE OFF WHILST YOU HAVE AN OUTSTANDING PENALTY AND REMINDERS IN FORCE."

Emilie lets out a frustrated sigh. She too throws her napkin down but onto an empty plate and gets up to leave.

Emilie lets herself into her apartment, looking dejected. Instead of talking to Emilie, Gina flashes up several large screens around her tiny apartment with text in red letters "YOU HAVE A PENALTY."

Emilie ignores this and throws her bag down on the bed. She picks up the Virtual Reality headset. Lars is in the park again and it is another lovely sunny day.

"Hi" he says in his usual warm, friendly greeting as he gives her a hug. "You're late today!"

"Hey you! I've had such a crap day."

"Why don't you tell me about it?" he says. They walk towards the shady tree they sat under yesterday. The sun feels pleasantly warm on her skin.

"Oh where do I start? I woke up late, missed breakfast, missed the gym and then over ate at lunch and again at dinner. My phone has been buzzing like crazy and I just had the worst date ever" she flops onto the grass. Lars however, is still standing.

His face has fallen from being happy to being alarmed.

"What happened?" he asked in a serious tone that she has never experienced from him before.

"I just had a couple of messages from Gina. She booked me in for a gym session tonight to replace the one from this morning but I went on my date instead. Dates in the real world are really hard to come by! I've been waiting months for approval." She says, unconcerned. "Gina says that I have to pay a penalty. I don't know what this is yet though." She says, looking at Lars, and shielding the sun from her eyes with her hand. Just then a dog barks in the distance, which is followed by a small child's laughter.

Lars looks frightened for her. She picks up on his mood.

"What? It's just gym and a couple of fines." She says.

"You need to get off here immediately. Go and sort this out now with Gina! If you don't, then the penalty is severe."

She looks at him. Now she is frightened. Her stomach is doing somersaults.

Emilie rips off the headgear and decides to do some research on the internet to find out where Lars is in the real world. He has never frightened her before like this.

"Gina, please display any information about Lars for me" she says urgently.

Gina completely ignores her. Emilie logs onto the database herself by docking her phone and starts typing on a projected keyboard like she has at work. She starts a search on information about Lars, and lots of articles pop up. In chat rooms people discuss him being a cautionary tale made up to make sure that you stay on the straight and narrow, whilst others discuss the possibility that he is there to be an outlet of pleasure so that people can enjoy the freedoms of the old days and still be productive in today's world. It would seem that many women and men fell in love with him and compared notes on what he was like in bed. She sees a newspaper article, written with the sensational headline:

MAN HAS ORGANS HARVESTED FOR HAVING AN OFF-DAY

Emilie reads and re-reads the headline. Her heart is pumping somewhere in her throat and her stomach turns over. She reads the next line.

A Sector G telephone operator was terminated for organ harvesting yesterday after he broke several productivity laws during a three-day binge

It shows a headshot of Lars smiling at the camera. It is definitely him, even though there is no mention of his name. Why didn't he ever say anything?

Emilie is shaking now. She sees another article relating to the 'Upper Levels' and that the people who live there were making complaints about having to wait on hold to talk to someone about their internet service provider. Her eye is drawn to a mental health publication with his photo attached to it. She starts reading.

Was this young man unlawfully punished?
A Sector G telephone operator was put to death because he broke a series of laws relating to productivity, but there is sufficient evidence to show that he had a mental health breakdown due to the gruelling schedule he was forced to keep.

Emilie re-reads the opening headline. She can relate to this. Her schedule is relentless and her quality of life is poor. She merely exists and is kept functional on a basic level so that she can work. She carries on reading the next few lines.

Every year over five million people are put to death in this way for breaking minor laws, yet the government does nothing to investigate why people are having breakdowns.

"The laws are there to be followed. He broke the law and he was punished accordingly" said a government spokesperson.

The journalist continues:

But what if there is a more sinister reason behind this? Say an organ donor shortage on the Upper Levels?

Emilie is mortified. She has no idea what the 'Upper Levels' are, but understands what organ donation would mean for her. Terrified for her own safety she clicks on the 'accept' button for "you have a penalty", hoping that it is not too late to sort something out with Gina. She inwardly pleads that she isn't beset by a similar fate to Lars. She hears nothing in response from Gina.

"Gina?" she says. Nothing. Gina is still giving her the silent treatment, and Emilie is feeling more and more anxious by the minute.

She carries on looking at the articles and comes across another government paper. This time it is a law document signed off by all 800 members of parliament.

Due to the serious infractions that occurred on 24th January 2142, it has now become necessary to reduce the time taken between an individual committing a crime and their punishment. Punishment will now occur within 24 hours of the crime. There will be sufficient warnings to give law breakers time to rectify mistakes within this time frame, meaning that it will only be persistent law breakers, deviants, and those who willfully subvert the law who will be terminated.

Emilie has another wave of adrenaline. This time it is followed by a jolt in her stomach as she hears a loud banging on her door.

"Open up!" shouts a man's voice, followed by more loud banging.

"This is Civil Compliance! Open up or we will break the door in!"

At that moment, all of the holographic articles disappear. She can hear Civil Compliance Officers ramming her door with something and hears a splintering noise as the door breaks.

"Gina?" Emilie says with a quivering voice "please help me!"

Emilie panics as she waits for the Civil Compliance Officer to arrest her. Tears are rolling down her face. I hope it doesn't hurt.

LOVE AND OTHER CRIMES
Written by Carmen Radtke

Peter stepped into the sonic shower. A short blast cleaned and exfoliated his skin. He rolled his shoulders back and forth and stroked his bulging biceps.

Extra gym session three times a week for six months, and the rewards kept coming in. To think he'd done a victory leap for something as banal as having dinner with a real-life human being when he reached his first 1000 merits.

The shower came to an abrupt halt. Peter patted his stomach. Solid muscle. He wondered what the girl from that date would think about his transformation. He'd always kept his body in good shape, but not like this. What was her name? Emilie? A strange girl, he remembered. Stuffing herself with cake even though it defied her parameters. She'd hardly noticed his presence, until he got fed up and walked out on her.

Funny, he hadn't seen her since. Maybe she'd transferred to another part of the city. It wasn't a real date anyway. A least not in the old-fashioned sense. Only the highest ranks got those.

He grabbed a bottle of musk-scented oil and massaged it into his body. Another brand-new luxury. Before his new fitness regime, he'd squeezed into a three by three shower with cold water, relying on nature to keep his skin supple.

Peter pressed a button on the central control panel, and his wardrobe slid open. "The navy-blue leisure-suit, I think." The rack rotated, and the suit dangled in front of him. He never tired of this.

His holographic cube hummed. A soothing lavender light spread over the surface, and a velvety voice said, "TEN MINUTES UNTIL YOUR SESSION IN WONDERLAND. ENJOY, PETER. YOU'VE EARNED IT."

"Thanks, Mary," he said. He blew the cube a kiss. 15 inches across, the biggest cube he'd ever seen. And his AI included personal messages these days instead of screening the standard appointment list. No doubt, his life kept getting better and better.

He changed into the leisure suit and settled down on the sofa, facing the waterfall in the jungle he'd selected for his personalised wall. He slipped the virtual reality mask over his head and relaxed.

*

Lana already waited for him by the lake. Every inch of her snowy silk dress clung to her curves. Her cherry lips curled into a smile that enchanted him every time he saw it. He broke into a trot, heart beating so hard against his ribs it hurt.

She held out her hands and pulled him down to the ground with her. It took all his willpower to settle next to her on the picnic blanket instead of covering her with kisses from the nape of her neck to her tantalising mouth.

Once a month they could indulge in such pleasures and more. Another fortnight to go.

Peter inhaled the soft scent of her skin. Roses, he thought. He'd smelled them before. A picture formed in his mind, the image of a slender dark-haired woman, and himself clinging to her with all the strength a five-year-old could muster. She'd smelled of roses too, his mother. A warm feeling filled the void the memory had left. She'd been a high-status girl, which explained the perfume and the fact that he'd been allowed to stay with her for a full five years. She'd be proud of him, and his achievements.

Lana dangled a fruit in front of him. "Try these, Peter. I got them just for tonight."

He nibbled the ripe cherry right out of her hand. "I wish I had a present for you," he said. "It's almost our anniversary."

She smiled at him, shading her doe-eyes against the sun. The rays were mirrored in the azure water, and painted golden streaks on her face. "I knew right from the start you were the one for me."

His fingers inched towards hers. Touching hands was allowed, even encouraged.

Almost two years, a relationship record as far as his real-life friends were concerned. Peter stroked her palm. Lana sighed, a lustful little noise that made the blood rush into his groin.

He got up, pulling her with him. "Let's take a walk."

A bird's nest nestled half-hidden in the reeds. "This is new," he said.

"You said you've got a bird on your wall."

Their fingers intertwined.

"You always make things perfect."

She moved so close her scent filled every atom of air around him. "You deserve it. You could have moved on a long time ago, when you received your intimacy licence."

"Never. I'll never leave you."

Lana reached out and traced his lips with two fingers. "Peter."

"Two weeks," he said, his voice husky in his ears. "Or less if I earn more merits."

They'd started out with a permission for sex every three months. Maybe one day he'd move up to being allowed to consume their love every time he visited, on his day off.

*

He took the virtual reality mask off. The cube hummed. "DID YOU ENJOY YOUR VISIT, PETER?"

"Yes. Yes, I did, Mary. Thank you."

"YOU HAVE 520 CALORIES LEFT FOR TODAY. WOULD YOU LIKE TO ATTEND THE COMMUNAL DINNER OR EAT IN YOUR APARTMENT?"

"He-" He broke off. "What is your recommendation, Mary?"

"SOCIAL INTERACTION OUTSIDE WONDERLAND, WITH HUMAN BEINGS, CAN BE BENEFICIAL."

"The communal dinner, please."

*

The dining hall filled enough space to warrant travellators running its length. Peter got off at the fourth stop in the left section and joined his co-workers and best friends, Mick and

Hans. Although sitting at mixed tables broke no rules, an unspoken law made the genders sit apart. The closest to physical contact outside Wonderland with a female that Peter had experienced was an examination. A short-breathed doctor had run a trial on his private parts a week ago. He'd felt embarrassed; dirty. Ten minutes in the shower hadn't been enough to get rid of that sensation.

Mick's glance wandered around. "Same old, same old, eh." He nudged Peter before he forked up another mouthful of mock beef stew. "Lucky if you can get away every single Sunday."

"You're just jealous," Hans said. He smoothed his thinning sandy hair back to cover the growing pinkness of his scalp.

"You bet I am. Six years working with you guys in the same call-centre, and all I ever got to was second base with my VR date, and she was a third generation holo." Mick prodded his food with a fork. "While others stick it in whenever they can."

A beep from his wrist-pad, and Mick flinched in pain. "Sorry, Gina, I won't use rude language again."

"You're still with a Gina?" Hans shook his head.

AIs, like the cubes or showers, signalled personal status. Marys ranked at least five levels higher than Ginas.

Mick glanced at his wrist-pad. "Gina only has my best interests at heart and looks after me relentlessly."

Peter and Hans grinned. The nice speech should make up for Mick's earlier transgression. Lower level AIs were less sophisticated than their higher evolved models. Mary would never let Peter get away with anything resembling irony.

He looked at his own wrist-pad and scrolled through the options for his calorie allowance. The mock beef stew looked good, with slices of onion and mock mushrooms floating in the sauce, but it came with dumplings, and he'd already had carbohydrates for lunch.

"What would you recommend, Mary?"

In public, she used the wrist-pad to communicate with him. "IF YOU WANT TO USE ALL OF YOUR ALLOWANCE, MOCK CHICKEN BREAST WITH SALAD AND JELLY FOR DESSERT WOULD BE YOUR BEST OPTION," the surface read.

"Is it better to use up my allowance, or to save some?"

"SAVING FOOD WITHOUT SAPPING YOUR ENERGY IS AN ACT OF GENEROSITY."

He had to stop himself from punching the air. "Please order for me, Mary, I trust your judgment."

He leant over to Hans and Mick. "You want to get ahead, cut some calories. And exercise more."

*

Three days later at dinner, Mick and Hans put a half-pint of beer in front of Peter. "Cheers, Peter." Mick grinned so hard the corners of his mouth almost met his ears. "This is from both of us. We didn't have enough left for a full pint."

They wouldn't, Peter thought as he breathed in the heady aroma of synth hop. He usually kept his alcohol allowance for the first day off after his monthly intimate encounter with Lana, to ease his longing. Two pints, that's how much he got a month. This, for Mick and Hans, was a huge sacrifice.

"What do we celebrate?"

"It worked, man, it worked. Hans has got a bigger cube."

"Bigger? It's like this. Enormous." Mick spread his hands eight inches apart. "I'm saving up merits to have you over one evening, so we can watch Community Spirit in private."

"And you, Mick?" Peter asked.

Mick lowered his voice although no one could overhear them, apart from their guardian AIs. "I got a friend. You know."

"Amazing." Peter slapped him on the back. For someone like Mick who most likely would never reach the levels of perks that Peter had, like his intimate meetings with Lana, a friend counted as one of the most desirable rewards to get. They came in all body shapes and colours, and the AI would activate them at the appropriate times.

"Have you already, ah," Peter searched for the right words, so Mary would not take offence, "well, tested her?"

Mick gave him a double thumbs-up.

Peter took a sip and let the beer slowly trickle down his throat. He pushed the glass over to Mick. "It's enough for all of us." He picked up his personalised water mug and raised it. "To our good services to the Community."

"To the Community."

*

Sunday, at last. The wake-up call roused Peter from his favourite dream, where he and Lana sat in the sunshine, and a little girl with Lana's golden curls and brown eyes lifted herself higher and higher on a swing. A dog chased a stick. Only the wooden cabin was missing from it being the perfect copy of a picture Peter had once seen in a travelling exhibition of now prohibited fairy tales.

For once he didn't mind waking from his dream. He'd see Lana tonight, and with his wealth of merits thanks to following Mary's every suggestion, maybe he could ask for a longer session already.

He made himself take his time over breakfast, chewing every bite for the recommended 20 seconds before he packed his gym bag.

The gym smelled of sweat, determination and in some cases panic, but Peter liked it like this. Every single effort where he exceeded expectations counted in his favour, and every bead of sweat made him a fitter, better part of this wonderful Community that rewarded virtue, loyalty and service to others.

He cranked up the pace on the treadmill. Voluntary sessions helped him pass the hours until he could put on his virtual reality mask and see Lana.

Soft music played in his ears, the beat perfectly matching his stride. One more bonus; voluntary sessions came with personalised music instead of the five standard songs of the compulsory training.

Another man gave up his place at a bench press. Peter slowed down, hoping that he would get there before anyone else beat him to it.

He wiped his brow as he got onto his back and reached for the metal bar. "50kg," he said. The weight automatically adjusted. Push, hold, down. Push, hold, down. "75 kg." Push, hold, down. Sweat slid down his temples. One last effort. "100 kg." Just stretching his arms with a weight intend on flattening him with agony. He pushed harder. "Enough."

He lay there for a moment, panting like the dog in his dream. He'd have to use the communal showers before he went to his apartment. Every muscle in his shoulders ached with that exquisite agony that came from a job well done.

*

Peter flopped onto his sofa. He'd have lunch in privacy, so he could daydream about the night ahead. Maybe they could go boating on the lake. He'd show off his manly skills with the oars, and Lana would lean back, her hand trailing through the water. There could be ducks to feed, or young birds to watch in that nest they'd seen.

"YOU HAVE EXCEEDED YOURSELF THIS WEEK," Mary said. "NOT ONLY IN YOUR PERSONAL ENDEAVOURS, YOU HAVE ALSO MOTIVATED OTHERS TO ACHIEVE HARDER FOR THE SAKE OF EVERYONE."

"Thank you, Mary." Peter tried to sound modest, because boastfulness and vanity ranked high among reasons for demerits, as well they should. Still, in his mind he made some quick adjustments to the mental image. Maybe he could kiss Lana. He felt her soft warm lips on his mouth, his throat, his – Mary's voice interrupted his train of thoughts. He instinctively covered his private parts with his hands before he crossed his legs.

"YOU HAVE THEREFORE BEEN APPOINTED ONE OF A VERY SELECT GROUP OF WORTHY MEN."

Peter sat as upright as he could, his gaze conveying trustworthiness as he looked straight at the cube.

"YOU, PETER, ARE GRANTED A LICENCE TO PROCREATE. YOU WILL MEET FIVE FEMALES UNDER SECLUDED CONDITIONS, AND IF ONE OF THEM SELECTS YOU AS THE FATHER OF HER OFFSPRING, YOU MAY THEN GO AND IMPREGNATE HER."

"I'll be a father?"

"IF ONE OF THE FEMALES CHOOSES YOU. IF YOU DO NOT FAVOURABLY IMPRESS ANY OF THE CANDIDATES…" A cube couldn't shrug, but that's what Mary's voice sounded like in his ears.

"A real woman. Outside Wonderland."

"YES. I HAVE ARRANGED YOUR FIRST DATE FOR THIS AFTERNOON. THE DETAILS OF YOUR PROCREATION LICENCE WILL BE STORED ON YOUR WRIST-PAD SO THE MOTHER CAN STUDY THEM AT HER LEISURE. YOU WILL TAKE THE ESCALATOR TWO FLOORS UP. RIDE THE TRAVELLATOR TO AREA 50 AND MEET THE WOMAN IN THE THIRD BOOTH IN THE EAST SECTOR OF THE ROMANCE PALACE."

The Romance Palace. He'd heard rumours about it, a restaurant with human wait-staff, music and privacy. They even had a wine list, with no restrictions for their customers, from what he'd heard. How he'd love to take Lana there and feed her real cherries before he'd whisk her home to their house by the lake. Lana. He swallowed.

"Does this affect my sessions in Wonderland?"

"WHY DO YOU ASK? HAVE YOU BECOME TOO ATTACHED TO YOUR VIRTUAL FRIEND?"

"No. Of course not." He forced himself to smile. While interactions in the virtual reality were designed to entice good behaviour in the real world, and for some people meant their only chance of seeing someone to have a laugh with all week, attachment was supposed to stay casual, to avoid addiction.

"GOOD. I'M GLAD TO HEAR THAT." Peter thought he detected a warning note in her voice. His left hand clenched.

"AS LONG AS NO FEMALE HAS CLAIMED YOU AS FATHER, YOUR WONDERLAND SESSIONS WILL BE FITTED INTO YOUR SCHEDULE. TO PREPARE YOU BETTER FOR YOUR PRIVILEGES, IT IS DEEMED WISE TO REFRAIN FROM OVERLY PHYSICAL CONTACT WITH YOUR VIRTUAL FRIEND. THE DOCTOR WILL TAKE OVER THAT PART OF YOUR PREPARATION."

He had to cross his legs again.

"Wouldn't it be advisable if I use the opportunity to prepare myself as much as possible?" He felt a surge of heat in his face. "I've been told that there is a certain - variety of personal preferences."

The cube changed its constant hum to something that sounded to him like pondering.

"WHO TOLD YOU?"

"So it's not true?"

"YOU MAY ENQUIRE FROM THE FEMALE WHAT SHE IS LOOKING FOR, AND THEN YOU MAY ATTEMPT IT IN WONDERLAND. YOU WILL ALSO SEND A MEMO TO ME ABOUT THE TECHNIQUE THAT I WILL PASS ON TO THE DOCTOR."

"Thank you, Mary. I hope I won't disappoint you."

"VERY WELL. YOU HAVE TWO HOURS TO PREPARE YOURSELF."

"Which suit would you recommend?"

*

He smoothed down the ruffles on his new black silk shirt. A velvet jacket in purple and tight black pants with added padding in the crotch made him look like a dandy from one of the few historic films shown on the cubes.

The clothes came as a surprise; new orders took at least a fortnight, so Mary must have felt very hopeful indeed.

Peter cast a doubtful glance in the mirror. What if the females rejected him? He'd get a maximum of two dates with each, in case he made it to the top two in a selection group. Should he be picked straight away, a man on the waiting list would fill his place.

A baby. A living, breathing, crying human being. He'd once held one in his arms, as part of the graduation ceremony. It served as a reminder of what bound them all together, and what one could achieve given the right attitude.

In all his 26 years Peter had never actually met anyone his age who'd fathered a child. His mother would glow with pride, he thought, although – did this count as cheating on Lana? Or, given that he'd used his new privilege to get permission to have more intimate contact with his love, was he cheating on a woman he hadn't even met yet?

He wished he could discuss this dilemma with another human being, but he couldn't risk it. If Mary found out about his attachment to Lana, that'd be the end of it. Not to mention the punishment for lying, and scheming to fulfil his own primitive urges.

The Community was merciful, but strict. There were always vague whispers about people who'd disobeyed the rules, people who vanished or were sent into the lower regions.

No; he couldn't risk it. He'd made it all the way to the top levels. Before the Change, when the sun shone benevolently on real lakes and proper grass and trees, he'd have had the house in his dreams. He knew that with every fibre of his being.

Losing his hard-earned place in society would be the end of him. He could live with a standard cube, and make do without the body oil and the sonic shower, but giving up Lana would break his heart. Mary could count on his compliance.

*

He checked his wrist-pad. Three stops to go until area 50. A moving shadow caught his eye. There, behind the thick plastic walls shielding the travellators, somebody had flitted past. Somebody with golden curls. The next stop came in sight.

Peter jumped off the travellator. He swivelled around, craning his neck. There, behind the barriers, a figure clad in grey ducked into what could be a maintenance tunnel. A figure with golden curls.

His wrist-pad vibrated. "WRONG STOP!" it read.

Peter winced. An exclamation mark, that came as close to yelling as Mary would go.

"Sorry," he whispered. "I just need to use a public facility."

He made a big show of relieving himself, in case Mary had him on visuals. He rearranged his private parts so the padded crotch bulged as impressively as he could ever hope and returned to the travellator.

*

The Romance Palace beckoned him with fairy lights twinkling in an artificial night. Glowing pebbles illuminated the path to the booths.

Inside the third booth, a woman reclined on a low settee. Artificial flowers crowned her dark braids. She smiled at Peter, revealing sharp little teeth, and patted the cushion next to her.

"Hi, I'm Adele. And you are – "

"Peter. Pleased to meet you."

His eyes adjusted to the dim light. A half-empty carafe with red wine and two glasses, and a buffet with half the olives and most of the cheese missing.

"Sorry, am I too late?"

"No, you're right on time." She noticed his confusion. "Don't worry, you're my third today."

"Your what?"

"Two ovulation periods, that's all I get, so Mary thought I'd better get cracking."

"Same AI." Peter felt himself warming towards her. "May I?" He reached for the wine.

"Plenty more where that came from. We all got a Mary. All of us compatibles."

The wine had a sharp bite to it, a little like Adele's teeth. She snuggled up next to him. Her hand rested on his knee, creeping higher and higher up.

"Why don't we move on to the important bits?" She blew warm air into his ear. "What do you have to offer?"

"A sonic shower. And a private music collection. Two dozen songs that I'm allowed to play every day."

"Nice." Adele's hand inched even higher. Peter stiffened. "But what else do you have for me?"

His voice caught in his throat. "Like what?"

She stroked his padded crotch. "I'm not buying blindly."

What would Mary want him to do?

She said, "Show me."

"I've never – "

"Peter, all I want is a look. Everything else," she rubbed her breast against him, "will have to wait anyway. I just need to see the goods, to get a feel for you."

He leant back, helplessly, as she unzipped his pants and slid a hand inside. The throbbing drowned out every other thought.

"Not bad." She touched every bit of him. "But don't you dare jerk off, like the other two. My doctor's told me exactly what I need."

The Civil Compliance unit. That's what he needed to think about. Civil Compliance, dragging away the degenerate from his desk in the call centre. He'd dribbled down his chin, yelling "Bastards" at the top of his lungs. Peter had to apologise on behalf of everyone to his customer, a lady who afterwards gave him feedback worthy of ten merits. Maud Delancy.

"Yuck." Adele sniffed at her sticky fingers. "Can you hand me water, hand sterilizer, and a towel?"

"I'm so sorry." Peter's insides knotted together. What would Mary do to punish him?

"That's okay. I guess. My doctor said this could happen." She grimaced, more resigned than anything else. "At least I didn't have to do the oral test on you."

"What?"

"Do you have visitation rights? In case the others also, well, you know."

He zipped up his pants, still embarrassed, and took off his wrist-pad. "You can check the details here."

She scrolled down the text. "You've got every Sunday off? And," she read the text again, "if suitable for my purposes you'd get an additional half-day a week to spend with us. I've seen worse."

He nodded, not knowing what answer she'd expect.

She nudged him. "I don't mean to be rude, but you're done for now." She sniffed her fingers again. "Definitely, I'd say. Take a sandwich for the way home."

"Right." He swallowed. "Can I ask you one question?"

"Well?"

"What would you expect from the male? Specifics." He pointed at his crotch.

She frowned.

"Please? It might improve my chances."

"Fair enough." She whispered in his ear.

*

"SHE WAS NOT RIGHT FOR YOU." The writing glowed on his wrist-pad.

"Thank you, Mary." His stomach unknotted. She'd forgiven him his lack of self-control.

"THAT MEMO WAS MOST GRAPHIC."

Oh, yes.

"STILL, IF THE FEMALE SAYS THESE THINGS PLEASE HER, THERE MIGHT BE SOME MERIT IN YOUR REHEARSING."

"I'll do my best."

"BUT FIRST, YOUR SECOND DATE. BOOTH SIX. YOU HAVE 30 MINUTES."

*

Another aesthetically pleasing woman, with almond-shaped eyes and honeyed skin. In the age before the Change she'd have been classified as Oriental.

The light shone brighter in this booth. The female stood up, and circled him.

"Good posture," she said, running her hands down his spine.

"I work out a lot."

"So I can see." She stood in front of him, a foot apart. "Sorry to be so brief but the clock's ticking for all of us. I'm Lily."

He shook her outstretched hand. It felt soft and firm at the same time, like Lana's.

"Peter. Just let me know what you expect from me."

She glanced at the sandwich in his hand.

"Why don't you eat first?"

He gulped the sandwich down in the shortest amount of time still compliant with the rules.

"I'm a first-timer," Lily said. "I need someone who will complement me genetically, so the child will inherit my sense of beauty and harmony, and the father will contribute physical perfection and patience. We would also need to have a shared sense of values, and enjoy each other's company."

She touched his shoulder, in a reassuring way.

"I design interiors. What does your wall show?"

"A waterfall, with the sun sparking glittering lights as it cascades down in a jungle of all kinds of shades of green. A bird with plumage in all the primary colours circles above it."

She squeaked with delight. "I can't believe it. That's one of mine."

"Then you can tell me what kind of bird it is?"

"It's a mythical animal, a parrot. It's said to have spoken with the tongue of man and crossed oceans on its adventures." She put her hand on his. "I like you. And your voice. It's kind."

"You're beautiful." An awkward pause. "I'm sorry, I shouldn't have said that."

"I liked it." Faint colour crept up her exposed throat. "But we'd better get on with business. What do you have to offer?"

He closed his eyes and grabbed the zipper. Lily stopped him. "Please. Anything less than perfection would have made you ineligible. Unless you – "

He shook his head, relieved. "No, that is, if you – "

"Once my decision has been approved, yes, but not before." She chuckled. "It appears that the lady in the other booth has different instructions."

"I'm not the first here."

She shook her head and held up three fingers.

"Have some wine."

*

When he left, she kissed him on the cheek, a kiss so light it barely registered before she clasped his face in her hands and kissed him again. Every conscious thought left him until she broke the contact and whispered, "I hope I'll be allowed to see you again."

*

He cantered onto the travellator. Lily; a lovely name for a lovely woman. The child would be beautiful too, with hopefully her hair and his blue eyes.

His memory brought up the dream picture, with Lana and the child. He tried to superimpose Lily onto it. He closed his eyes. Someone bumped into him. His eyes flew open as he steadied himself. Three stops from the restaurant. He thought he saw another shadow crouch past behind the barrier. Maybe -

Mary demanded his attention. "YOU WILL NOW RETURN HOME IN TIME FOR YOUR WONDERLAND SESSION. THE NEXT APPOINTMENT AT THE RESTAURANT WILL BE TOMORROW NIGHT, AFTER WORK, SO MAKE SURE YOU PRACTICE THE REQUESTED TECHNIQUES."

He made a quick calculation in his head. "Would it be advisable to walk the last part of the way, instead of taking the travellator to the restaurant?"

"FOR WHAT REASON?"

"Additional exercise, so my body will be limber but not tired."

"ACCEPTED."

*

Bird song filled the air as he arrived at the lake. Lana broke into a run as she saw him, and he caught her in his arms and whirled her around.

"I've missed you so much," he whispered in her ear. You could never be sure if Mary or another AI didn't listen in.

"Now you're here." She hugged him a little tighter. "Come and look at the birds. They've hatched, all five of them. A little family."

Her words hit him like a punch in the guts. A family. He'd once heard someone say that the people on the lowest levels were allowed marriage, and children, and they kept the kids instead of handing them over to Community nurseries. All to replace workers at a quicker rate, the bloke had said. No, not said; he'd screamed it. "Fodder for the working mills," he'd marched around the dining hall, banging his fist on a metal pan that rang like a gong. "You know why you won't have any children? No-one needs more idiots with implanted head-sets." It took two civil compliance officers to subdue the lunatic. Still, the words haunted Peter.

Lana crouched down, next to the nest. Five birds, with plumage so thin he could see the prickly skin underneath. They stared at him, unblinkingly, while their yellow beaks opened wide enough for him to see the veins in their throats. An older bird sang his heart out. Peter saw a tear form in Lana's eye.

"What do you do when I'm not around?"

She drew in her breath. "I wait for you."

He teetered dangerously close to the edge with these questions, but somehow he had to know. "But what do you do? How do you fill in the time? Or –" he hated himself for doing this to her. "Do you have other visitors."

"No. No!" She clutched his hands. "When you're not around, everything is like – I don't know. As if I'm drifting in a dream. You're my reason for being, Peter. Don't you want me anymore?"

"Sorry." He pressed kisses on her hair, her forehead, her cheeks. "I'm so sorry. I just – I have permission to be with you tonight. Properly, I mean. If you want me to."

*

The sun set over the lake as he got dressed. They always shared this, a picture of a fiery ball sending out waves of orange, pink and yellow ripples reflected in the water. The birds fell quiet, as Peter closed his eyes and left Wonderland with an aching heart.

Mary woke him an hour early the next morning, to fit in the gym session that he'd normally have had in the evening.

She was very quiet, he thought, ominously quiet. The cube shimmered yellow, signalling unease.

"Have I done anything wrong?"

A slight pause. He felt his breath quicken.

"YOU ARE POSITIVE YOUR ATTACHMENT TO YOUR FRIEND IS WITHIN THE PERMISSIBLE RANGE?"

She must have watched them. "It is."

"YET – "

"I apologise for interrupting you, but you can't wish me to be so unkind to make my friend feel used." He took all his remaining courage together. "Would that hurt a friend's feeling? Unless - do they have our kinds of emotions? Or are they all AI like you, there to steer us gently towards aiding the greater good?"

He hoped she didn't notice the rise in his body temperature. These questions bordered on heresy.

"YOUR THOUGHTFULNESS IS APPRECIATED," Mary said. "ALL FRIENDS ARE INDEED EMOTIONALLY ENABLED AND MATCHED AT THIS MOMENT TO SUIT YOU."

At this moment? "Then I must thank you for arranging my contacts with human and AI friends."

"SHE'S NOT AN AI. HURRY, YOU NEED TO BE IN THE GYM IN FIVE MINUTES." The cube switched off.

Peter made it through the day on autopilot. In his mind, he mulled over the same question, until his brain felt foggy. Lana was not an AI. She must be real. How could he find her? His thoughts went back to the girl with the golden curls. Was it Lana?

*

He performed his plan to get off the travellator at the last possible moment, bumping his knee on the exit barrier so hard he bit into his hand to stifle a cry.

He strolled along the same direction as the shadowy figure had the day before. If he was honest, he didn't know why he was doing this. Well, yes, the figure might have had golden curls like Lana, and he had been curious, but it couldn't be her. He'd always tried his best to comply with the rules. So why, all of a sudden, did he find himself breaking them?

Love, he thought. The love he felt for Lana, the love he felt for a baby that he might father. What was so wrong with that concept that the Community wouldn't let everyone have that?

His right shoe hit a metal bar. Peter came to an abrupt halt, one hand against the wall to prevent a fall. He hated these shoes, with their shiny rubber but Mary approved of them.

At the bottom of the wall a finger-wide gap showed next to one panel. A golden hair was stuck in it.

Peter's curiosity kicked in again. Later, he told himself, if he found a way to lose his wrist-pad for a bit. But first, date number three.

*

A compact female, with an aggressive chin and a firm mouth.

"I'm Peter," he said, holding out his hand. She ignored it.

"You're blond," she said.

"Yes."

"Pity. Your credentials?"

He took off his wrist-pad and put it on the table.

"May I?" He motioned towards the wine.

"Half a glass. If you must indulge."

Not much sympathy there, he thought. His spirits lifted. The thought of having to let her in his pants had made him feel queasy. He drank faster than usual, as she read through all the details, muttering under her breath.

"Sorry," she said, dropping his wrist-pad, "but you're so not what I want. Don't waste any more of my time."

He hung his head, feigning disappointment and dashed off, leaving his wrist-pad behind.

Hopefully this would buy him enough time to take a closer look at the wall panel.

The hairs on his neck bristled as he slid his fingers inside the gap and pulled. There was no one around, he told himself. People used the travellators. These sidewalks might have been populated once, but these days only maintenance workers could be expected here, and their shifts ended an hour ago.

He lowered the panel onto the ground. It gave a small plonk as it hit the rubber-concrete mix. Resources were finite in the Community, and recycling was writ large in the rules. Everything had a purpose, from hair to stuff mattresses for the poor, to faeces. That fertilised the hydroponic beds.

The gap was wide enough to fit a body. Inside his crotch padding he'd hid bandages. He wound them around his knees for protection and slid inside, before he could come to his senses.

He'd expected darkness, but diodes alongside the echoing tunnel gave off enough light to see the strands of cables running all the way. He crawled past a side opening.

The bristling got stronger. A prick in his neck, and then everything went black.

*

He came to in a small room. Tight rope secured him to a metal pipe. A girl with golden curls watched him with something bordering disgust. Lana? An elderly man stood next to her. His legs were bowed, but he looked like a fighter.

"What unit are you on?"

The man flicked a knife open and held it under Peter's chin.

"Mary."

The man gave the girl a questioning look. She pulled out a button-covered pad and typed a command.

"Five minutes," she said, with Lana's voice. Peter stared at her. There was the same generous mouth, the way her hair grew into a tiny widow's peak, but she had a tiny mole on her left cheekbone. A small sound escaped his throat.

The man touched Peter's jugular with the blade.

"What are you doing here, clown?"

"I saw you yesterday. I thought you were –" Moisture welled up in his eyes. "I thought you were Lana."

"What did you say? Who's that?" The girl's soft voice grew a sharp edge.

"My friend. In Wonderland."

"What's that?"

"Virtual reality? Everybody knows." His voice faltered. No wrist-pads. These people wore no wrist-pads, and their clothes were unfamiliar too.

"You're fugitives," he said. "I've heard stories."

"Like what? That we eat children and grannies?"

The man pulled back the knife far enough to convulse with laughter without killing Peter.

"Lana. You were telling us."

"She is – I love her. Please don't tell my AI. I don't know what she'll do if she ever finds out."

"I could tell you." The girl looked him up and down, as if to fully weigh him up. "What were you going to do once you found her?"

Peter shook his head. He had no idea. "I only wanted to see her. Be with her. Not just every Sunday for a two-hour session by the lake."

"Sounds romantic."

"You've got no idea, do you? I work in a call-centre, six days a week. I go to the gym, I donate calories, and all the time I think about her. And now I've got a licence to father a child, and these females check me out and use me."

"Must be tough to be a sex toy."

"I want a baby. I want to be a father, and I want Lana to be the mother." Tears ran down the sides of his face. The girl wiped them off with her sleeve.

"I thought she's an AI, a hologram or something. But I asked Mary, and she told me that Lana's real. She exists, but Lana told me that she only really is awake when I'm around."

The man whistled through his teeth. "The high security ward."

"What?"

"You don't know anything, do you? They've got a hospital on the outside, and they've got one down here. Here's where they do the dirty work."

"There is no outside. It's all contaminated."

"You really believe that? Outside, that's where the power is. For now."

The girl said, "It's true. I've been there often enough."

"So Lana is alive?"

"Her body is. I guess."

"I need to find her."

The girl gaped at him. "Are you crazy?"

"She looks like you."

"I don't care what she looks like. We can't save her. Not yet."

Peter shook his head. The ropes cut into his flesh.

The man said, "Can you buy us another five minutes?"

The girl nodded and took out her pad again.

"One wrong word from you, and they'll kill us all."

"I would never betray you," Peter said.

"Oh yeah? Procreation permit, sounds to me like somebody's been a right little boot-licker."

Peter grew hot. "It's for the greater good. What's wrong with that?"

"Depends on who the greater is, but that's just my opinion. Personally, I don't like it when people are killed and gutted so someone rich can have a shiny new pair of eyeballs or a new liver to pickle."

"That's enough," the girl said. "He's got no idea."

"What are you talking about?"

"You're better off not knowing too much." The girl said.

"Lana. Is she in danger?"

The girl averted her gaze. The man shrugged. "Could be. Her brain's probably hosting all kinds of different holo friends. Two hours a week for you, leaves plenty of time for someone else. As long as she's useful and not self-aware, she'll be fine. Otherwise..." He ran a finger across his throat.

Peter gagged. "I need to find her."

"You can't. You wouldn't last longer than five minutes."

She put a cool hand against his cheek.

"I'm sorry, but you shouldn't have come here."

"You're going to kill me?"

"We're not monsters. We're going to make all this go away. You've never seen us. What's your name?"

"Peter. Peter 47, apartment 201 on the top level."

"If we find her, we'll come and get you. Until then, be a good slave. Play by the rules, enjoy your time with the ladies, have that baby."

"Can't I stay with you?"

"Live in hiding?"

"Yes."

"You wouldn't see her again. Ever. They'd pull the plug on her or at least wipe her brain."

Peter's insides turned to mush. "What have I done?"

"It's fine. A little prick, and the memory of us will go away."

She shoved a piece of cloth-covered wood in his mouth and clamped a metal ring over his head. The pain seared through his body. He bit down on the wood until the splinters dug in his gums. Then he went limp.

*

He stared at his wrist. No pad. He must have forgotten it at the Romantic Palace. Sweat formed in his armpits. Mary would be upset. He broke into a trot.

The female had gone, but his wrist-pad still rested on the table. He clasped it to his chest. "Thank you, thank you, thank you." Theft happened hardly any more in the Community, and an AI would notice immediately if an unauthorised person used a wrist-pad, but things could get lost.

Angry letters formed on the screen.

"WHERE HAVE YOU BEEN?"

"I'm so sorry, Mary. The female, she, she rejected me and told me to go at once. I…"

"I HEARD IT ALL. THIS DOES NOT ANSWER MY QUESTION."

"I walked, and then I noticed that I'd left my pad behind."

"NO MORE WINE FOR YOU."

"No, Mary."

"YOU HAVE TWO MORE APPOINTMENTS FOR TOMORROW. DON'T MAKE ANOTHER MISTAKE. AND NOW GO FOR YOUR DINNER. HAVE YOUR FULL ALLOCATION. MOCK BERRIES AND FISH. IT WILL HELP YOUR BRAIN-FUNCTION."

The letters vanished.

*

Hans and Mick had almost finished when Peter arrived at their usual table.

"What's happened to your sunny smile?" Mick said. "You look like you ran into a wall."

"Have you upset our AI?" Hans frowned.

"I'll make it up to her." Peter typed his order onto the table-pad.

Mick peered over his shoulder. "Berries and fish? No wonder you've got a face like somebody weed in your beer." His wrist-pad zapped him. "Ouch. Sorry, Gina."

Peter's food arrived. The mock fish resembled pink blubber, and the berries weren't much better. He had to force the food down.

"So, what happened?" Hans lowered his voice. "Did you do it?"

"Do what? Oh." Peter cringed. "How did you know?"

"Your wrist-pad. Mary is all-powerful and wise, but discreet, no."

"Do we have to talk here?"

"No." Hans grinned. "As soon as you've finished your feast, we'll have a boys' night and watch the cube at mine. I've got pretzels, so you want to save some calories for that."

*

Hans' apartment had a much smaller feature wall with a sunset over a mountain range, but it felt cosy. The new cube rested on a Perspex plinth, facing the sofa.

Peter, Hans and Mick had to squeeze in tight, but they'd done that for as long as Peter could remember. He relaxed. These were his friends, real friends.

Hans snapped his fingers, and the cube sprang to life. Community Spirit was the longest-running series in history, with daily reruns. They could just let it wash over them in the background.

"Tell," Mick said, catching a pretzel with his open mouth.

"It was, well, weird." Peter felt the blood rush to his private parts again.

"Like, forbidden stuff?"

"Of course not. But honestly? You're not missing out on much. Wonderland is better. So's Mick's friend at home."

"Yeah, right." Mick's voice was barely audible thanks to the cube. "How does a real woman feel like?" He squeezed Peter's chest.

"Don't know."

"What?"

"It was just like at the doctor's, okay? I wasn't allowed to touch. I'm not even sure if one of them will pick me anyway."

"Sure they will." Hans winked. "Best piece of manhood around, if we aren't in the running."

Mick suddenly went serious. "Don't blow this, okay? You're doing this for all of us. Hans and I will be able to say, there's a child running around here that our friend has fathered. Come the revolution…"

They chanted in unison: "…which will never come because the Community is supreme."

"Well, having a child means you'll always protect it. You'll protect them all because each of them could be yours. Peace forever."

Somehow for the first time in his life that argument left Peter unconvinced. His mind had trouble focussing. Mary was right. He'd cut down on his food too much; it weakened his brain.

But he'd make it up again. Tomorrow he had another two dates, and with any luck Lily would select him as her partner. If not, it didn't really matter, as long as Mary understood. Because every Sunday, he had Wonderland, where Lana waited by the lake.

OLD TREES DON'T BEND
Written by Emma Pullar

I've been above for a while, a very long while actually, more than half my life, but I still remember the darkness – that pitch black what used to happen when the lights tripped out. Many still live it, right under my damn feet. I know it's wrong that I'm up here and they are not but who am I to question it? I've never forgotten my days on the lower levels and I never want to go back down there. Not ever.

Sunlight penetrates the transparent walls of the glass box I've worked out of for the last fifty years. Palm on the lockpad, I stare into the light, entranced by the tiny particles floating in the brightness like fallen stardust bewildered by their descent to Earth. I lean in, press down on the pad and the creaky greenhouse door which has a tendency to stick, judders open. My stooped silhouette is cut out against golden brushstrokes which fan across the well-trodden floor. Shadow leading, I step over the threshold, and a wall of heat hits me. As I move further into the humid box, mud trailing in from the bottom of my boots, the sun climbs up my frayed, forest green dungarees until it reaches my face; it warms my weary skin and pushes a smile to my lips… that is until I reach for my gloves and the dawn stretches out its fingers and pokes me in the peepers.

"Bots alive!"

I drag down my government issue visor from atop my balding head and cover my squinting eyes which begin to un-squint, opening back up like a snail's does after it's shrunk away from someone's touch. I tap the adjuster at the side of the visor. The inside of the greenhouse is a blur. I tap faster, if I wasn't wearing the visor anyone looking at me might think I was tapping the side of my head in an attempt to wake up my brain; if only they had a gizmo for that. The lenses finally come into sharp focus. Ah, technology, sometimes it really is a blessing, these old eyes aren't what they used to be and without the visor I wouldn't be able to give the attention to detail that young Maud demands of me.

I scoop up the grey gardening gloves I left on the bench yesterday evening and with some difficulty, I wriggle my hand into the left glove. I always struggle to pull on the right one and today is no different. I pinch the thick fabric with my gloved hand but there's no strength there anymore. The glove flops to the floor.

"Oh bugger!"

Back creaking like the greenhouse door, I stoop to retrieve the glove. I straighten up as much as my bowed spine will straighten, and pick at the soil-stained material, the fingers worn and rough.

"I'll never get this poxy glove on." I curse and toss it across the bench. One glove is better than no gloves, I suppose.

Reaching across with both hands, I pull a terracotta pot towards me and examine the lollipop shape growing out of it. It's almost ready for planting, few more snips and it will be as uniform and un-tree looking as Miss likes. I turn the pot with my gloved hand and admire my work, a perfect sphere… just a minute! One of the roses has wilted. I lift the open bud with my other hand.

"Blast!"

I snatch back my arthritic claw. There's hardly any feeling left in my fingers but prick myself on a thorn and I feel it all right. Nothing like bloodletting to get the circulation going, it's a timely reminder that I'm not dead yet, even though there are some who want to force me to rest, to cut back my hours. I won't. Do that and I might as well get in my coffin now. Not that they use those anymore. Can't bury the dead underground with the living. Anyway,

I'm only seventy-seven not ninety-seven. There's still life in this old tree yet.

I suck the red from my thumb and a faint metallic taste swims over my tongue, along with traces of bitter potting mix. I spit the grit and my lips vibrate, making a rude noise. The sound reminds me of my wife. All she seems to do these days is blow it out the backend. She is forever apologising for it. I always smile at her rosy cheeks, flushed with embarrassment and tell her she's full of hot air. She giggles like a school girl. I love her as much today as I did when we first met forty years ago. She's my reason for living; her, my two adult children, my little granddaughter and my gardens. Technically, the gardens I tend aren't mine but in my mind, they are, they're my pride and joy.

The first garden I tend each day is always Maud's. I've known Maud since she was a nipper but I can't say I have much affection for her, I tolerate her because she's the reason I get to breathe unfiltered air and bask in sunlight. Would I choose her for company or friendship? No. For me, a savage dog with a tendency to bite my arse every time I meet with it would be more fun. What does she want these rose trees for anyway? What's wrong with a good old-fashioned rose bush. Half the work and twice as pretty. I hate these new-fangled plant hybrids, especially all these weird colours. Rainbow roses, I mean, why? It's not as nature intended, is it? But then the disaster changed everything, the plants are not the same as they were before, or so I've heard. I wiggle my thumb and a red line runs down my hand.

"Hang it all!"

If I ask for another plaster she'll think me incompetent, she already thinks I'm getting too old to do the job. I search the greenhouse. What can I use? There's a familiar shushing sounds to my left, like the pumping of an old-style inhaler. It's not that though, it's one of those things! I wish she would stop sending for more. I don't need them. They get in the way. Revolutionary, my wrinkly arse!

A round red light, like an evil eye, flashes up on the front of the bot's metal body as it speaks.

"FOR. THE. BLOOD."

The voice isn't robotic but it isn't free flowing either; it sounds like a woman reading slowly from a technical manual so a student can understand. The mechanical creature, which has eight pointy legs and is reminiscent of a spider, holds something white in its pincers. Daft machine, what is that? Some new even slimmer feminine product? Blooming things can never tell male from female. It's got its wires crossed, I need a plaster!

"FOR. THE. BLOOD." It repeats and will keep repeating these words until I acknowledge it.

I reach out, take the white strip and wrap it around my thumb, it clings to my skin and dissolves, sealing the cut.

"What is this stuff?" I ask the bot.

It doesn't reply, it scuttles across the bench and goes back to dropping seeds into a tray. I know better than to ask it again. It won't answer me. Productivity, productivity, productivity is what the bots are about. It only stopped to patch me up so I could go on being productive. They're creating new innovative things all the time. This new strip the bot gave me must be the latest wonder. I scrutinise the spider-legged machine for any differences, any sign of an upgrade. Does this one has a camera in it? It's possible Miss Maud is watching from up there in her palace, spying on me, making sure I'm earning my keep. I'm still useful. These bots can't think for themselves, they're programming is limited. They wouldn't know how to save a withering plant, they'd just rip it out and plant a new one. No care. No ingenuity. That's why Maud needs me around.

"John!"

Her shrill voice shoots me in the eardrum, causing my heart to bounce against my ribcage, I place my hand over my chest to calm it.

"Yes, Miss?" I answer and scan the greenhouse, where is she?

"Come up to the house at once!"

I look for the voice and sure enough, it's coming out of that new bot. Not a camera inside it but some sort of communication device. Nasty metal spy. I pull off my glove and hurl it at the bot. No emotion, no senses, it doesn't move, just waits for the glove to hit it and then shakes it off and carries on dropping seeds in the tray. Miss normally sends one of the lawn boys to get me, at least I get to talk to another human being that way. A thought strikes my mind like a match being lit. How long has Miss Maud been listening to me through that bot? Did she hear me swearing earlier? Perhaps I'm in trouble for cussing.

"Ouch!"

Sharp pain to my ankle. The crazy bot with the missing legs (the one I think might follow me home one day and do me in in my sleep) clings to the right hem of my dungarees. All the mechanical bugs are creepy but this one is creepiest, not only is it bat-shit crazy but it scuttles with a limp and makes weird clicking noises. I once dropped it in the recycling bin but it managed to escape and I'm sure it's never forgotten. I shake the deranged bot from my ankle and it skids across the greenhouse floor. I kick the little sod out of my way and press my palm to the lockpad; wondering what I've done or not done, this time.

***

The maroon painted steps curve from the house entrance like a giant, lolloping tongue. Place one foot on it and be dragged into the belly of the mansion, which looms over the grounds, pointy turrets like a crowned goblin, its grey stony face chipped and cracked. It was once grand and Maud expects us to see it as it was when it was first built, we're all supposed to marvel at its grandness, but for me, it's a monstrosity. It's meant to be elegant but isn't; like the lady of the house herself, who wears dresses that remind me of used wrapping paper – shiny and bright but a bit crumpled here and there. Despite what's inside the wrapping, a fit, young body, I imagine, she's a present nobody wants. Perhaps that's why she's on her own. A job's worth is what Grace says about her, an entire week's worth of jobs is what I think. Thankfully, she can't read my thoughts, at least I hope she can't. I sometimes wonder.

I shan't be using the steps up to the house, they're for show. I don't think anyone has ever used them. I'll be taking the travelator. There's a secret door to a secret tunnel to the secret entrance to Maud's mansion. It's not just for staff, everyone uses it, even Maud. I don't use it often, only for important announcements, like the time she wanted the orchid moved. It took me nearly an hour to explain that gardening isn't like decorating, I can't just move established trees around, they're rooted to the earth. Another time I was summoned to the mansion was because she wanted to scold me for planting the wrong colour marigolds. I tried to explain to her, that unlike trees this problem is an easy fix but oh no, to her the world was ending, she would have the same over the top reaction if her dresser hadn't matched the right pair of shoes with her outfit. Born air-side, she doesn't know about the dirt-dwellers. If only someone would give her a taste of it; just one week of strict routines, controlled diet and exercise and no natural light, perhaps she'd be less demanding and a tad more grateful after a week down there.

I approach the hole in the hill, right hand held against the base of my back; it's playing up today, pain shooting like knives pushed into my spine. I wonder if the backache is a result of all the forced exercise from when I lived dirt-side.

I'm sure it did more harm than good to push my body to its limit, sure I was muscular and at the top of my game but now I'm paying for it. Although, I wouldn't change anything, that's how I made it air-side, it was worth it just to feel the sun on my face and breathe fresh air.

Desi is on the door. Desi is always on the door, does Desi ever leave here? As I approach the stocky android; shoulders square, visor over her eyes, (I don't think I've ever seen her eyes, maybe she doesn't have any), I notice she is not standing in her spot, she's about two inches closer to the wall. Strange. I would ask her why she's moved but I'd get no response. She doesn't talk, I've never heard her voice. I always speak her name in greeting anyway.

"Desi." I nod, trying not to look like I'm holding my aching back but rather strolling casually, hand on my hip.

She jerks her head downwards and nods back. Then, body unflinching, her arm automatically lifts and presses the lockpad on the wall. The double doors slide open for me to pass through.

***

The tunnel is a weird place. It smells of damp, mothballs and rotten wood. I don't like it. It reminds me of my old life, even fifty years on the fear of being back there still haunts me. My old Eve Unit, which was basically a snitch in a box – a gizmo to make sure the lowers stick to their rigorous schedules, drove me bonkers with its continuous commands and the only saving grace (I think of my wife) was that it could also provide information about any subject. I always chose to learn more about plant life and drank up the knowledge like a thirsty child gulps water. That's why I was chosen. When they checked my AI Unit and found I'd been researching horticulture I was selected for a special recruitment programme, there were several of us in fact. I'd been working my way up to the top level or so I thought, and I had no idea what was about to happen. Five hundred and fifty years is what they told us, the surface would be uninhabitable for that long. They lied. I've often thought of getting word to the lowers but then the dread sets in, the leak would be traced back to me, I can't risk it.

Standing still while the travelator moves you along is an odd sensation in itself, especially because it's on a slight incline, I have to shift my feet several times to maintain my balance, but coupled with Maud's eclectic taste in ornaments and decorations, it somehow seems even worse.

I feel like Alice tumbling down the rabbit hole (or rather up, since I'm heading up to the house) and each time I come through here there's more junk what's been added. Abstract paintings of the garden, I can only imagine Maud painted herself. They're not bad, I guess, lots of brush stokes resembling trees and flowers. The tacky part comes in with the fairy lights and lanterns draped from painting to painting, and skinny round tables topped with curiosities and fetishes (ugly useless things) he tables are placed exactly the same few feet apart (she probably made the staff use a ruler). I eyeball each one as I pass, to see if there's anything new been added to her collection. There are statues of people in fancy clothes, decorative plates and vases and... what's that? A skull with a hot pink afro and a pipe poked through its missing front teeth. It's like travelling through a museum of clutter and crap that no sane person would ever want. I wonder where she found all this stuff?

At the other end of the tunnel is a thick metal door. I press the pad on the wall and wait. A buzzing sound jars my senses and the doors swish open and disappear inside the wall. I step through into the foyer and the mothball smell is replaced by a whiff of lemon cleaning agents. The great polished statement reminds me of a building I once saw a projection of – The Acropolis of Athens with its huge towering pillars. I shuffle across the sprawling marble floor, weaving my way through the pillars, careful not to slip. The floor is shiny enough it reflects my lined face, thinning grey hair (visor perched on top) and silvery trimmed beard. How did I get so old so fast? I don't feel the way that I look. Except for the creaking back and nagging arthritis, that is. Something brushes up against my leg. I reach down and scratch it behind the ear.

"Hello Madam Whiskers."

The white pedigree cat purrs loudly as I tickle the side of her squashed in face. Her furry features are as flat as a board like the cats in them old cartoons; as if she chased a mouse across the foyer at top speed, it got away into the mouse hole and then unable to stop, Madam Whiskers' face crashed into the wall, flattened forever.

"Come through, John!"

Maud's shrill voice echoes around the foyer and up into the high ceilings.

I tread carefully as I make my way to Maud's sitting room. A strange name for a room. A place dedicated to sitting doesn't seem like a luxury to me, how boring.

"What's taking you so long?" She squawks. "Come in and sit down."

"Sorry Miss." I say, ducking into the modern room filled with exotic antique furniture. The far double doors are open, breeze pushing the netting and patterned curtains around playfully. I take my place in the straight-backed servant chair. "How may I be of service?"

Maud sits in an armchair reminiscent of a throne. Her legs are pressed tightly together and swept to the side. I wonder if anyone has ever been brave enough to venture up her dress, god knows what she's got hiding under there, some sort of bear trap ready to snap down hard on any man who gets too close. She's too proper to get sweaty, too prim to be naked in front of anyone, probably does it with the lights off. I keep my stare level with her head, her breasts are pushed up so high any man would be forgiven for dropping their gaze but I don't let that happen, I stay fixed on her creamy-skinned stern face and auburn hair clipped up with diamonds. She hasn't acknowledged me yet, a woman's face projects from her AI Unit, it flickers and crackles. The snitch in a box sits on the table like a centre piece, it's the latest model, a Pandora, which is apt since Maud thinks of herself as a goddess and if she was told not to open Pandora's box, she definitely would.

"Thank you, Rose. I'll ask for him when they call back," Maud speaks with a plum in her mouth, the voice reserved for her friends is a lot posher than the tone she takes with me, "trouble is, these 'techies' sound like they're calling from down a hole..."

I turn away, worried my face will tell her the truth. What would she say if knew about the lowers? Would she believe me? Would she even care?

"Bye now." she kisses the air like she's kissing her friend on both cheeks and the flickering image evaporates, "Ah, John! Thank you for coming to see me."

She smiles at me, or rather she pushes her cheeks up with her red painted lips, teeth not visible, she hardly ever shows her teeth.

"Of course, Miss." I nod.

"I wanted to let you know the party will be here," she says, pouring a cup of tea from a china teapot small enough it could belong to a child's play set, "it's all arranged."

"Party, Miss?"

"Yes, the party."

I raise my eyebrows. I don't know how to reply. Maud tilts her head and sighs, the tiny gemstones in a line from the corners of her eyes glisten as her head moves into a shaft of sunlight.

"Don't play dumb, the formal notification was sent today and as your employer, I was also notified. I've ordered more bots to compensate, so you needn't worry about me."

Why would I worry about her? Delusions of grandeur, much? She lifts the cup and saucer, then holding the saucer with one delicate hand, she takes the cup to her lips with the other and sips the steaming tea. She doesn't offer me a cup. She never has, I don't know why I would expect her to now. I scratch my head.

"Beg your pardon, Miss. I don't follow." I say, and grip the arms of the chair, nervous I've forgotten something else, I brace for a telling off.

"Your birthday will be your last day, and it's only fitting I throw the party, since the lion's share of work is done for me, I don't expect Ms Bradberyl or that pretender Toddly will give you a good send off, not like I can."

Send off? My heart stops. Am I dying? Did she get some medical report about me I'm unaware of? Grace must have got it. I've got to go home!

"Thank you for your generosity, Miss, but there's no need for a party, seventy-eight isn't a milestone birthday."

"Now, now, John. I've never known you to be stubborn and seventy-eight is actually the most important milestone in a worker's life."

What on Earth is she going on about? My mouth hangs open, I manage to purse my lips enough to form a word.

"But…"

"But nothing! It's settled, I've already sent the invitations," she takes another sip of tea, leaving a smudge of red lipstick on the white china, "Saturday at four, don't be late!"

"Yes Miss." I say, holding back a sigh of frustration, "Will that be all?"

I can't believe she brought me all the way up here to tell me she's organised a party for me. I don't know why she would want to bother, she's never done anything nice for me in all the years I've worked for her and neither did her father before her.

"Do we ask such questions of our employer, John?" Maud sneers.

"No, Miss and I hate to be a bother but I'm a bit behind on my duties now."

"I see," the china clatters as she places the teacup back on the saucer, "in that case, you'll come in half an hour earlier tomorrow to make up for it. Where are you off to next?"

"Ms Bradberyl, I'm ashamed to say I forgot to run an errand for her this morning."

"Oh John, that's no good, you'll get your rations docked again. You're rather forgetful these days…" she taps her forefinger to her ruby painted lips, nail polish the same colour, "hurry and get it done, it's best to go out on a good note."

Stone the bots! Go out on a good note? I don't feel unwell; how can I be dying? Poor Grace is probably tearing her hair out with grief over that notification.

"Right away, Miss."

I hurry from the room, leaving her ladyship to finish her tea. Madam Whiskers waits by the door for me, meowing as I pass. I stroke her soft back a few times and she leans into my touch. The poor cat is starved of affection. I don't think Maud even likes cats. The only reason she has one is because it's seen as a status symbol. With most animals extinct, a cat, especially a pedigree one, is a rarity, reserved for those privileged few who can afford to buy and care for a pet.

I leave Madam Whiskers in the cold foyer and force my aching bones to move faster. I lied about the errand for Ms Bradberyl. I'm going straight home to my wife.

***

When I reach my cottage, which like me, is old and creaky, Grace is waiting, back up against the open front door. Her shift doesn't start until after lunch, her hours were cut back once she hit sixty but not by much, nurses are always sought after. The cut back was enough that we could have lunch together every day. There was a time, in our youth, when we worked so many hours we hardly saw each other, it was the only way to keep the children fed, rations don't go very far and seem to get less and less every year. Grace must have known I'd come straight home when Maud delivered me that news. I scan her face as I approach; trace around the smiles lines and crow's feet and up to the frown lines between her eyebrows. Our eyes meet, she doesn't seem sorrowful, she seems exasperated, frustrated, I don't know. She's never been easy to read.

"Did you see the notification?" I ask, no time for a greeting kiss or hellos.

"Come in and see for yourself, John."

Grace moves into the cottage and I follow. The smell of tomato soup drifts from the kitchen and my stomach rumbles as if a hungry animal lives inside it but I can't eat, I can't even think straight. Our cottage is not much bigger than the greenhouse. In the tiny living-room, our worn-out android – the old 8th edition, a gift from Maud, she probably didn't want to pay to have it recycled – is perched on an even older wooden chair, beside the small dining-room table. There is this saying: 'On its last legs' meaning almost ready for the scrap heap. The synthetic's legs haven't worked in two years, unable to replace them we removed them. This rare robot, reserved for elite air-siders, (although I've only ever known Maud to have them, since they come from daddy's factory), had Annie printed on the back of the neck, short for android we guessed. The children adored her, she's a member of the family. They've tried to issue us with an AI Unit but I hate those cubes, always watching ya, I'd rather fix up Annie and because she still works, they don't bother sending a cube. I fear we won't be able to keep her running for much longer, and perhaps, like Annie, I'm on my last legs too.

"HEEEEL-LOOO, J-JOHN."

Annie's once human sounding voice is now an electronic mess of drawn out words and glitches.

"Hello Annie." I say and take a seat across from her.

Annie's synthetic eyelids flicker and her head wobbles as she struggles to sense where I am.

"I'll go get lunch, we'll have it early." Grace says and hurries from the room.

"I H-HAVE A NOOOO-TIFIII-CAAA-TION. FOR YOU."

"Thank you, Annie, please project." I say, heart pounding. Stay calm, John.

Words blink up and project from the cracked screen in Annie's stomach area. I lean across the table and read as fast as my ability allows. I read well enough but sometimes my mind trips over longer words or words I've never encountered before.

Notification For: JOHN HERBERT PARKER

Work Grade: GARDENER

Age: 77

Notice: RETIREMENT

Travel Needs: TO BE ESCORTED TO RETIREMENT FACILITY

When: SATURDAY

Time: 6pm

I flop back in the chair and let out a deep sigh. I'm not dying, it's much worse than that, they want me to retire. What's a retirement facility? Is that where Sam and his wife went? We certainly never saw them again, how old were they? I thought they'd just moved town. No one has ever mentioned a retirement 'facility' to me. My forehead crinkles in thought; *wasn't there a news report not long ago about the retirement age being raised?* I hit my palm to my head in an attempt to jog my memory. I'm sure they said eighty-five so why am I being retired now?

Grace reappears with a small basket of bread rolls under her arm and a bowl of steaming soup in each hand. She sets them down and Annie immediately offlines; head down, body still, projection gone. Grace takes a seat beside me, worry etched into her kind face.

"Well?" She says wringing her hands.

"Well, what?" I say, dragging a soup bowl towards me.

"You're leaving Saturday." She says, bottom lip quivering.

I reach across, place my hand on hers and give it a gentle squeeze.

"I'm not going anywhere."

***

"If I could just talk to someone in charge…"

"TAP ONE FOR NEW ADMISSION DETAILS."

"I already tapped one. I want to talk to a person!"

"TAP TWO FOR A LIST OF PROHIBITED ITEMS."

"For goodness sake!"

I mash all the numbers projected from Annie's stomach screen with the palm of my hand, she doesn't move, she's on downtime while I make this enquiry which is good because I don't want her to know what I'm doing, I don't want Grace to worry.

"TAP THREE FOR…"

I frantically jab all the projected numbers with my index finger.

'I just want to speak to a person! Is that so –

A hologrammatic face blooms from Annie's screen and lights up the dark living-room as well as my face but unlike sunlight it emits no heat. The pale face blinks at me and then its thin lips start to move.

"Good Evening, you're through to Mitchel, reception attendant for the Retirement Facility, how may I attend to your needs?"

"Hello Mitchel," I address the floating head, "I need help with the admission process, and please don't transfer me to someone else, I've been cut off several times already."

The floating head smiles.

"I can help you with that, give me your name."

"John Herbert Parker."

"Thank you, John. You are due for admission on Saturday. Please arrive at the facility promptly at six."

"That's what I'm calling about, I want to withdraw my admission for retirement. I'm quite happy to continue with my duties and stay in my home with my wife."

The talking head raises his eyebrows.

"I'm sorry, John, you misunderstand. Retirement is not negotiable. Please report to the facility on the date and time specified. Good day."

"Wait!"

"Do you have another question?"

"Yes, there was a news report, it said something about the new retirement age rising to eighty-five and –

"If I may interrupt… the new retirement age applies to citizens under forty, you are not under forty."

"Okay, but is there any way in which you can talk to your boss or your boss's boss and explain to them that there really is no need for me to retire –"

"No, John, Retirement is a requirement. See you Saturday at six. Good day."

I throw a punch at floating head, my fist falls through it and the image disappears, leaving me in darkness and despair.

***

Saturday comes around fast. I've never understood why something you don't want happens at speed while something you do is slow in arriving. Maud certainly didn't spare any time or expense in organising this send off. The garden is decorated with strings of fairy lights, just like the ones in kleptomaniac tunnel which leads up to the house. There are little clothed tables dotted about the lawn with ribbons tired around the chairbacks, reminiscent of a wedding rather than a garden party. She'll use any excuse to have a gathering. The grey clouds overhead threaten to ruin her fun and I welcome it. *Go on, rain on her parade.*

I scowl at the holo-banner which flashes up with the words: 'Happy 78th Birthday, John and a Merry Retirement.' Maud's put on a spread and even had a cake made - a huge replica of her garden. It isn't a cake for me, it's another way of showing off – showing off to her guests – a reminder that she's not rationed or restricted, she does whatever she pleases. The party is filled with her wealthy friends, the only people invited from my life are my family. Grace, my son and daughter and my five-year-old granddaughter, Dot. Maud slinks up beside me. She wears a feathered dress with plumes that might once have belonged to a peacock, if they ever existed, I'm pretty sure they're a mythical bird.

"Do you like it, John?" she asks, gazing at her handiwork; the banner, the cake.

"I'm eternally grateful for the extravagant birthday party, Miss," I say, straightening my jacket (my only suit jacket) and forcing my fake smile as I have done on many occasion, "but I'm not retiring."

"Oh." Maud says, feigning interest as she glares at a couple at the back of the garden, getting rather too touchy feely under a tree.

"I've decided not to go," I say with as much confidence as I can muster, I've never decided anything before, up until this point all decisions have been made for me, "I'm more useful here and they're raising the retirement age, so…"

She's not listening to me.

The couple notice Maud's hot stare and break apart. Maud gives me her full attention, her smug painted on smile looks as if a child drew it on with a red crayon.

"With all due respect, John, your work has gotten sloppy over the years and you're no longer as useful as you were," she says these mean things but keeps smiling as if she's complimenting me, "that's why I have the bots, they'll take over from you, so you needn't worry, you can enjoy your retirement safe in the knowledge your good work will be continued, and it'll be even better than you did it."

She's loving this, spiteful cow!

Maud slinks off, distracted by the arrival of a tall and suave guest in a navy suit. I look down at my tan trousers, worn at the knees, they don't match my green jacket. A bot scuttles along the cake table and drops something in front of me, it's covered in dirt. I pick it up and shake off the soil. It's a ring. It's a bit bent but I'm sure that's what it is.

"Where did you get this?" I ask the bot.

"FERTILISER." It replies in that irritating stagnant tone.

"How would a ring get in there?"

Idiotic machine!

"RING. IN. PLANT. FOOD."

"Useless metal menace."

I take a swipe at it and it scuttles away. I sigh and prod the misshapen circle of silver in my hand.

"What you got there?"

I flinch and discreetly pocket the bent ring.

"Nothing, my darling." I say to Grace, who looks radiant in her 'only for best' floral dress, 'bit of rubbish a bot found in the garden.'

I gaze back up at the flashing sign and Grace seems to read my mind.

"You knew about retirement, John. Everyone knows." She says, rubbing my arm to comfort me.

"I thought it was optional, Grace, not a requirement." I say, but who am I trying to convince, her or me? Did I really think that or have I been deluding myself all these years?

"How many people do you know who have opted not to retire?" She asks me, knowing full well what my answer will be.

I think hard, my eyes instinctively move to the side of the brain that retrieves memories but I can't access any, I don't know anybody who stuck around and stayed in their job after the age of seventy-eight. I can't think of a single person.

"But Grace…" I hold my wife's slender hands and look into her eyes, the one part that hasn't aged, they sparkle like they always have, she tries on a reassuring smile, yet those beautiful brown eyes are tinged with sorrow, 'I don't want to leave you.'

"Pop pops," my granddaughter tugs my trouser leg, when I look down she stretches her tiny arms up to me, "cuddles."

I shouldn't lift her, my back will give out, even so I squat down and use my knees to straighten up. I swing her onto my hip, she wraps her tiny arms around my neck and her curls tickle my cheek. I hold her tight, pressing my hand against the back of her frilly lemon dress. I can't do this, they can't make me leave my family. *Suck it up, John. They can always visit.*

"The officers are here, John."

Maud is flanked by two tall, muscular, Civil Compliance officers. Why do I need two? Are they taking me to prison? The officers stride towards me and Maud joins my family.

"John Herbert Parker?" I nod, "We're here to escort you." The male officer says. No smile. Stony faced, like someone dragged him to this party after a bad break up. His female counterpart is much the same. Probably trained not to smile. I take a step closer to the female, Dotty's arms and legs still clamped tight around me.

"Before we go," I say gently, "you need to give my family the address."

"Address?" The female officer says confused.

"So they can visit me," I say, "I know it won't be often but–"

"It won't be at all," the male officer smirks, "you're going to The Gates."

I frown.

"But there's nothing at The Gates, except…"

The realisation hits me like a speeding truck. I can't go back down there! I won't see my granddaughter grow up. I'll never see my son and daughter ever again. No visitors down there. Too risky. The lowers might find out about the surface and then what? Mass migration, chaos, civil unrest, but I can't leave my family, I can't just walk out of their lives and forget about them. I'll never see the sun again. What about gardening? It's all I know.

"Let's go, John." The male officer grasps my arm.

"There's no need to touch me!" I spit, my son lifts Dot from me and she starts to cry.

"Don't cry little Dot," I coo, "Pop pop is okay."

"Goodbye Dad," My daughter steps in front of the officer and embraces me, head nestled into my chest like she used to when she was Dot's age, my bottom lip trembles when her wet tears sink through my shirt, she pulls away and wipes her eyes with the backs of her hands.

The officer yanks my arm. Rage bubbles up.

"I said let go!"

He doesn't, he yanks me to comply and follow him. Grace rushes forwards.

"I love you, John." I cup her face with my hands and kiss her soft lips, the officer tugs me again and we're broken apart.

"Grace!" I yell and mouth, "I love you too."

My son cradles a crying Dot while my wife and daughter hold each other and sob. The other guests don't know where to look. Maud wears an expression of pure delight at the drama unfolding. Was this her plan? Throw me a party because she knew I would make a scene, make her dull life exciting for a fleeting moment. She doesn't even know what's under her feet, ignorant bitch! She has no idea where I'm going, years of loyal service and for what? The years of forced obedience catch in my throat, about to erupt from my mouth. Well, if she wants a show, I'll give her a show!

"I said let go of me!" I shout and tug my arm away from the officer, his counterpart rushes over to restrain me.

A fire lights behind my eyes, I could take on ten men. The female officer reaches for my other arm, I elbow her in the chest and she draws back, not quick enough. Arm up, fist clenched, back punch. Her thick nose cracks. She cries out and drops like a sack of fertiliser.

Gasps and whispers rush around the crowd but no one moves, no one intervenes, they huddle together like a frightened flock of hens and watch me struggle. Pampered princes and princesses stare on in shock. *Oh sorry, have I upset the balance? Have I upset your perfect little lives?*

"It would be wise to comply." The officer growls at me.

He holds both of my arms in a vice-like grip. In a flash of fur, Madam Whiskers leaps onto the officer's face and digs her claws deep into his skull, he yelps in pain as she bites his face and kicks and scratches him with her back legs. He releases my arms, and grabs for the cat. I'll not let him hurt Madam Whiskers! I jab my knee up between his legs, the cat leaps away from the danger and the big fucker hits the ground and rolls around beside his co-worker, holding his crotch.

I rush towards my family. No plan in my head, we need to run, get away, go into hiding. My wife wears an expression of grief. There's a tug to my trousers and this time it isn't my granddaughter. It's Limpy, the horrible little fucker! One after the other, spider bots clamber up my legs. I fall under the weight, my back slamming hard into the ground. Grace whimpers but no one comes to my aid. My son, who is the sensible one, must be holding them back, he's thinking of their rations and how I wouldn't want them to starve on my account but I do, I want us all to starve together, someplace else, somewhere away from their rules. The bots' sharp pincers puncture my suit trousers and scratch my skin as they scramble up my body as if they mean to devour me. I bat one away but it recovers quickly and resumes its scurrying.

I manage to grab hold of one by its round metal body. I throw it like a tennis ball at the male officer, who's back on his feet. The bot slams into the officer's angry face and clings to his cheek, he grunts when sharp legs draw red marks down his pale skin as it struggles to grip his fleshy cheek. I throw another one and its round metal body clonks the other officer on the head.

"Fuck you!"

"John!" Grace gasps.

I've got nothing to lose no more. The knee of repression lifts from my broken back, the flood gates are open.

"Fuck all of you! You can't do this! I've been loyal. I've served loyally!"

"John," Maud pipes up, her face puffed up like a red balloon, I've obviously gone too far, even for her, "calm down!"

They can't arrest me. I won't leave my wife, I won't leave my job. I'm not going back down there with those dirt-dwellers! I'll die first! I struggle against the scuttling garden bots as they scramble over my aching body and pin my arms and legs to the ground.

"Desi!" The male officer beckons Maud's bodyguard with a wave of his hand.

Her robotic legs stamp towards the officer at an even pace, her head facing me. No, I shake my head, she won't betray me. She'll get these things off of me.

"Help me, Desi." I plead with my eyes.

Surely, she has some attachment to me. After so many years of working in the same place, there must be a flicker of emotion inside her. She can't be the same as these things holding me down. She almost looks human, they must have given her some sort of emotional range. Desi gives her attention to the officer and he whispers something to her in close quarters. The android turns her head back towards me, her body follows and once close enough, she offers me her hand. I take it and she pulls me to my feet, almost pulling my arm out of its socket. The garden bots fall to the ground and start scurrying around, confused.

"Thank you, Desi, thank you." I say, shaking her synthetic hand.

"Take him away!" The female officer orders.

Desi grasps my hand tight. My eyes widen. She can't.

"Go with her, John." Grace pleads, tears falling down her soft cheeks, "It won't be long until I'm with you."

"It'll be ten years, Grace!" My voice cracks, "We haven't been apart for more than ten days."

The android I've known for five decades drops my hand, steps behind me, grips my shoulders and pushes me forwards, away from my family.

"Desi, stop!" I cry out and crane my neck to look back at my wife, "I can't be without you, Grace. Please! I can't breathe without you."

Grace drops down on her knees, face buried in her hands as if she's crying over my grave. Maud is quick to put her arm around my wife's shoulders, fake comfort, she's enjoying every minute of this. She'll be gossiping to that bitch Bradberyl and anyone and everyone just as soon as I'm gone.

My arm is yanked up behind my back and I trip over my own feet, legs twisting around each other like the tangled roots of a tree. I stumble forwards. Desi holds my arm so tight I can almost feel my skin bruising, my back creaks and crunches but she doesn't let go, she's doing her job. I grimace in pain but there's no emotion from the synthetic, she doesn't loosen her grip. Desi drags me, the years of nodding to each other at the hill tunnel were meaningless for her. Seeing me almost every day means nothing to this android, she's not like Annie.

I twist my body and dig in my heels.

"I won't go! Old trees don't bend, I won't bend!"

For the first time, Desi speaks, her voice is robotic yet sickly sweet.

"OLD TREES DON'T BEND…" She forces my arm into an impossibly angle and I scream when the bone snaps. "…BUT THEY DO BREAK."

To be continued…

GET A JOB
A Civil Compliance Message

PRIVILEGE

Written by Carmen Radtke

The silence came as a relief. Maud shuddered for a second at the memory of those piercing shrieks from John's pathetic wife as Desi dragged him to the door. Who'd have thought that such a small frame could hold so much noise? The whole family had scuttled away as soon as their stubby legs allowed. They even left the cake behind that Maud had ordered especially for her gardener's farewell party.

Ingrates. She turned to her guests. "Music," she said. An invisible orchestra filled the room with violin and piano sounds. "So much better, isn't it?"

Her remaining guests, all of them old friends, broke into insincere smiles. Only Rose declined to join in. Her mouth formed an o, as if the impression that John's removal had caused stayed with her long after he'd gone.

"Why did you do that?" she asked.

"Do what?"

"Your Desi hurt him, and he's an old man."

Maud frowned. "He brought it on himself, refusing to leave with the Civil Compliance men for his retirement. You can't blame me for that."

A thought popped up in her mind. "Of course. He looked after your garden, too, didn't he? No need to worry, darling." She put a manicured hand on Rose's shoulder. A tiny chip on the left pinkie marred the perfection of her jewel encrusted nail varnish. She eyed it with growing irritation. She'd call the company in the morning and complain about the manicurist. If the girl didn't take pride in her job, she shouldn't work at Heavenly Nails. But she mustn't let herself get worked up. Frowning caused wrinkles.

Maud increased the pressure on Rose's shoulder. Rose stepped back a few inches, to reach for a chocolate that the maid offered around.

"I have the perfect solution." Maud allowed herself a chocolate, too. They were made solely for her, after her own design. Maud admired the swirls indicating sunrays, and the golden glitter sprinkled on top.

"Together with the lawn boys, my bots are capable of everything you could want, Rose. Just say which models you need, and I'll make sure you will be put on top of the waiting list."

"Is that why you got rid of John? So the bot factory could increase sales, and your shares would rise?" Rose's voice, which could not be called dulcet at the best of times, rose to an unpleasant pitch, piercing through the music.

"He'd reached retirement age, as you perfectly well know." Maud fought hard to keep her annoyance in check. "I begin to regret giving this party at all. But if you do want to make a spectacle of yourself ..." She pressed her fingertips to her temples. She could feel a headache coming on.

She should have invited that dishy doctor after all. Or she could call him, once everyone had gone home. Maud closed her eyes as she recalled his perfect features, and that slim, well-toned body that the white coat hinted at when he examined her. What a pity Lucas had been born on the wrong side of the tracks. The men of her own sphere were fast becoming inbred dullards.

"Desi hurt him," Rose repeated. "Your amusing relic, as you call that thing, broke his arm."

"The Civil Compliance unit would have done a lot worse. And they gave the instruction." Maud flicked the thumb over the chipped nail, faster and faster.

Another guest chimed in. Desmond. Of course it would be that sycophant Desmond. Anything to get into Rose's good books, or her silk knickers. "I thought no AI was allowed to harm a human."

"They are not, and Desi didn't mean to harm him. It's an old unit, and the movements never were as smooth as my grandfather hoped when he designed it."

"But it is dangerous." Desmond shifted his flabby body as close as he could to Rose.

"Don't be ridiculous. My AI unit has it perfectly under control." She forced her lips to curl upwards at the corners. "It's unique, the only surviving of the three Desi units my family built. And now, if you'll excuse me, the party is over. Good night."

She swept out, aware of all those gazes following her. It didn't matter. The maid would see them all out, and take care of the clean up with the aid of her darling bots.

Idiots, all of them. She should just have let Civil Compliance remove John after his final shift in her pleasure gardens. Too soft, that's what she was. Too generous.

She felt a sharp stab in her liver.

"Pandora?"

"YES, MISTRESS MAUD, WHAT CAN I DO FOR YOU?" her AI unit, another prototype connected with every wall in her home as well as her diamond pendant, asked.

"Please run physical diagnostics."

Her pendant throbbed gently on her bare skin. Diamond had excellent conductive propensities, her father told her. How lucky to have such an illustrious lineage of AI and bot designers.

The name Maud Delancy stood for generations of public service and innovation. That was something people like Rose didn't understand. Privilege carried with it responsibility. As if she would ever let John go for her own benefit! The very idea reeked of selfishness. A few more remarks like that, and Rose could find herself in an awkward spot with the Ministry of Civil Compliance, in which Maud held an inherited position of importance.

Madam Whiskers sneaked closer. "Good cat," Maud said, hoping the flat-faced creature wouldn't insist on coming closer. Cats, as children, should be seen from a distance and best not heard at all. She could thank her rarity value that Maud let her sleep in her private quarters. Madam Whiskers, irritating as the white Persian was, could never be replaced.

The cat yawned, as if to show Maud that she too could not be bothered to fraternise. They had a delicate balance of mutual indifference.

Another stabbing pain in the liver distracted her.

"YOU APPEAR TO HAVE DEVELOPED A SENSITIVITY TO WINE AND CHAMPAGNE AGAIN," Pandora said.

"So soon?"

"Shall I arrange for another transplant?"

Maud ran her hand over her ribs. Most high-ranking families suffered from inherited organ weakness, thanks to the genetic damage inflicted by the poisons that polluted the atmosphere only a handful of generations ago. That's how she met the dishy doctor, when he examined her to find the ideal liver for her physiology.

"Could they open up the old scar again?"

"ONLY THE DOCTOR WILL BE ABLE TO TELL YOU. OTHERWISE YOU COULD FOREGO ALCOHOL."

"Let us do that for a few days."

"As you wish, Mistress Maud."

*

Maud leant out of her window. The crescent moon, rarely seen through the clouds and remaining layers of pollution, sent a glimmer into her garden. The pink and purple pulsing lights lining the winding staircase and the meandering pathways illuminated the rose bushes and the rainbow of orchids planted in an octagon around them.

Maud felt her forehead crease. She stroked the skin until the lines disappeared. John had broken off two branches the last time he pruned the roses. It had taken all her willpower not to yell at the old fool. Good riddance to him. Her father had seen something noble in John. His ebony features reminded Dad of a wooden statuette he'd seen in a minister's house.

Maud drew her silk kimono tighter around her breasts. If her father had seen the old gardener these days, he wouldn't have been able to detect anything noble in those gnarled claws. As for the ebony skin, it had taken on an unpleasant greyish tinge that made her detest his presence in her immaculate surroundings. Dirty, that's how he looked like. As if the soil he dug in day in day out, had taken over his skin and every cell in his body.

The sheer nerve of that man, to defy her orders, when she told him which plants she wanted in her newly created terrace beds. "It's the soil that gives the marching orders, Miss Maud," he'd said. No, it bloody well wasn't. She smiled to herself. She gave the orders around here, and only she. When she consulted Pandora, or John until today, it stemmed mostly from courtesy.

Her hand wandered towards the cooling unit. She always kept two bottles of Champagne in there, chilled to a perfect 55 degrees Fahrenheit, with 70 percent humidity.

The face of her mother appeared on the gleaming steel surface of the cooler. "YOU INTENDED TO FOREGO ALCOHOL FOR SEVERAL DAYS," the face said with Pandora's voice.

Maud withdrew her hand. "And I will."

Maybe it had been a mistake to use that face for her private chambers. Tomorrow she'd have it reprogrammed with another picture. A parrot, or a lion.

A happy chuckle rose in her chest, despite the alcohol deprivation. Because tomorrow she'd receive her latest, and most spectacular acquisition. Two living, breathing and hopefully breeding birds. The aviary would be erected in the early hours, with a canopy including ray filters shielding it from harmful emissions.

Birds! A shiver of anticipation woke up her dulled senses. She'd only seen half a dozen of those creatures in her thirty-eight years. Nobody would believe the amount of favours she'd had to trade in to gain access to these elusive creatures. All the strings she'd pulled would probably reach halfway around the planet.

She sighed as she slipped under her silk duvet. Just as privilege had its responsibilities, so did responsibility carry with it a certain privilege.

*

A Strauss waltz broke Maud's sleep. A wheeled bot five inches higher than her bed made its way across the polished oak floorboards. On its surface stood a steaming bone China teapot with a blue and gold willow pattern, a matching cup and a plate with scones and fresh plums.

Maud slid up higher in her bed and plumped up her pillows so she could rest comfortably. She poured her tea and sipped it while planning her day. Her liver felt much better. No need to call the dishy doctor after all.

Maybe she should run into him in his spare time. Pandora could get his shift details from the system. Pandora could get anything. All the AI units were connected, including the decrepit old Annie that she'd donated to John when her father passed away after his fifth heart transplant.

Maud put the cup down and reached for a scone. Funny how nostalgic John's retirement had made her. The Annies, like Desi, had been failures, useless attempts at marrying human form with the electronic brains of the hive mind. People found them creepy – possibly because of their almost life-like appearance. Still, the company had produced thousands of Annies.

Maud helped herself to another scone. That was something she sorely missed, a person who shared her interest in artefacts and relics. Her collection of antiquities, like this teapot, and Desi, and the skull with the pink wig in her hallway that she dusted herself daily, held an unrivalled place on this planet. Or at least it would, if Maud should ever feel inclined to make it public.

She poured herself more tea. Nine o'clock. Most people of her strata would now be sweating in the gym, or preparing for yet another hospital treatment, or study available partners for cementing their position by marrying into the right kind of family. How boring it must be to be them.

She certainly intended to do none of these things.

"Pandora, call Image Corp. I want Peter on the phone." Her mother's face reappeared on the wall.

"YES, MISTRESS MAUD."

A small panel slid out of the wall panel next to her bed. A button glowed. Maud pressed it.

"Peter here, Ms Delancy." The young man sounded soothing as always. She tried to imagine him. "What can I do for you today?"

"How tall are you, Peter?"

"Five foot ten, Ms Delancy?"

"And your hair? Your eyes?"

A tiny pause, then he said, "I'm blonde, with green eyes."

"Good looking?"

"I couldn't say, Ms Delancy. I hope at least I wouldn't offend your eyes."

She snuggled into her pillows.

"Can you remove the reflection of my mother's face from my AI unit and replace it with yours? I know it's unusual, but somehow I'd feel more comfortable with some of Pandora's suggestions if they came from – someone personable."

"In that case, why don't you personalise the image? I can patch through some possibilities, and help you with the design. That would give you a face that is yours to look at and yours alone."

She smiled. "Excellent. I knew I could rely on your good sense."

Maud wondered how old Peter was, and where he lived. There was something in his voice that appealed to her senses. A hint of freshness, and innocence, and physical peak-time.

Blank faces flitted over the wall, faces with a narrow or a jutting chin, differently shaped ears and eyes.

Maud settled on a slightly rugged male face, with brown curls that fell into the forehead and begged to be smoothed back, a cleft in the chin and brown eyes like molten chocolate. A face she wouldn't mind to order her away from the drink.

"Thank you, Peter," she said after he'd downloaded the face into Pandora's system. "I will let your supervisor know how helpful you've been again."

He laughed. "It's always a pleasure to be of assistance to you, Ms Delancy."

What a pity Peter didn't live close enough to be accidentally met, too, she thought.

Only the highest caste and those in their service, like the dishy Doctor Lucas, lived in the neighbourhood. Maud wasn't quite sure where all the others dwelled, but not here. She deliberately avoided all Ministry and subordinate Council meetings dealing with these details, because she did not want to be accused of amassing too much power.

She could happily live with the status of being the richest woman, and the physically most desirable and unreachable one. There was no development in AI technology that she didn't have access to, and had she so desired, she could have her organs exchanged on an hourly basis.

The face, the new face, spoke again. "THE AVIARY WILL BE READY IN HALF AN HOUR."

Maud frowned. The face was perfect, she wouldn't mind undressing in front of it night after night, but the voice no longer fit.

"Get me Peter again, Pandora."

"AS YOU WISH, MISTRESS MAUD."

This time she had to wait for three and a half minutes until Peter was free. "We need to adapt the voice," she said.

"What kind of voice did you have in mind?"

She paused. Stern? No. Patient? Again, no. "Firm," she said. "With sex appeal and a hint of authority. A bit like yours in a few years."

"You flatter me."

He patched through a few sound samples. Maud closed her eyes as she listened to them. The third one sent shivers down her spine. "That one," she said.

"Certainly, Ms Delancy."

"Oh, and could you put me through to the complaints department of Heavenly Nails?"

A metallic clank came from the other side of the line. "Sorry," he said. "I dropped my stylus. I'll put you through straight away. Have a pleasant day."

*

Five minutes later Maud hummed to herself as she dressed in a pink and red pantsuit. The girl who wrecked her nails would learn how costly sloppiness could be. Two hundred merits deducted, and no VR time for a fortnight.

Maud inspected the tiny chip again. Barely noticeable, but it was there. Not acting on it would have been aiding and abetting the girl in her slovenliness.

So many duties rested on her slim shoulders.

*

Three workmen waited at the side entrance for instructions. In the door, blocking it, stood Desi. It amused Maud to see how respectful the men – all of them almost too well-fed, and at least six feet tall - treated the old machine.

"Step closer," she said. "Desi won't bite."

"Yes, Ma'am." The oldest of the trio, a hulking man with a tattooed bar code that classified him as out of date and unlikely to progress, twisted his cap in his oversized hands. Black hairs sprouted from the knuckles.

"Have you never seen a unit like her?" Somehow it pleased Maud to think that she introduced these walking muscles to something akin to culture and refinement. "Desi was meant as an experiment, to see how close to us AI could come."

She laughed, a carefully modulated trill designed to put inferiors at ease. "This, I admit, was always doomed to fail. As useful as our programmable helpers are, they will never equal the dexterity, sense of innovation and empathy the human race has been blessed with."

"No, Ma'am," the cap-twister said.

Maud risked a side-wards glance at his companions' arms. Barcode-free, and no wrist-pad. That meant they had the ID implant, which also included a location tracker and the basic memory for its carrier. Why didn't their spokesmen have one?

She shrugged mentally. Not her business. She clapped briefly. "You have received the instructions?"

The man pointed behind. Large panels made of gilded metal bars and grooved wooden planks littered the ground. Maud glared at him. "I will have no rubbish left behind, is that clear?"

All three nodded, gaze firmly on Desi.

"Follow me." Maud swayed on her high heels as she wove her way along the intricate crazy paving that snaked around the upper part of her pleasure gardens. "Pandora, please remind me that the paving is too smooth."

"YES, MISTRESS MAUD."

The men lagged behind, lifting the first couple of panels high enough not to touch any of Maud's shrubs and trees.

Her gaze fell on a blade of grass poking out between two paving slabs. She pursed her lips. No, better to wait until the men had finished before she sent out the bots. The workmen could otherwise be relied on to trip over her metal helpers and crush something vital under their big bodies.

She swayed her hips a bit more, mindful of the admiring gazes she knew rested on her pert bottom. "Look all you want," she thought. "This is as good as it gets for you."

She stopped at the bottom of a path, under an old tree with curiously shaped leaves. There should have been name plaques for her flora, she thought. One more thing to be added to her ever-growing list. She could not possibly be expected to show guests around and introduce them to a tree with curiously shaped leaves.

"This is where you will build the aviary," she said. Far enough from the house not to disturb her should birds make noise, and close enough to be seen out of her bedroom window.

"The what?" The cap-twister gaped at her.

"Good grief. The metal structure, you moron. I'll be back once you are finished."

She turned sharply, only to find one spiky heel stuck in soft earth. This was getting intolerable. What a pity that John was out of her reach, or she'd have told him what she thought of his negligence. The soil needed firming down, and the paving was too narrow to give her the freedom of movement she needed. She'd have the lawn boys extend it.

An acidic taste crept into her mouth. She forced herself to count backwards from fifty and calm down.

"TWO HOURS UNTIL THE BIRDS ARRIVE," Pandora said.

Two hours! She needed a bath, a massage, and her meditation time. This was to be her day of glory, the day when she became the proud owner of two almost extinct animals. Redbirds, or Cardinals if she remembered correctly from the manual Pandora had played for her a week ago.

The bird keeper was still due to arrive. Maud had insisted on a man. They provided so much more delicious diversion than a female, especially when they were young, with strong arms and a smooth, broad chest. By now the labour distribution department knew her requirements by heart. They'd learned their lesson when they tried to foist a scrawny lawn boy with more acne than face on her.

The man would sleep in a hut next to the aviary. She had insisted on constant availability. Nothing was allowed to possibly go wrong with her precious birds. She'd keep an eye on them, and on the bird keeper should he prove to be worth it. Otherwise she could rely on Pandora using the bots for unrelenting surveillance.

*

The birds took her by surprise. Their red plumage matched her nails – she really needed something done to the chip - but instead of being the imposing creatures she'd expected, they could sit on a teacup.

The feathers formed a peak on their head, and their small button eyes watched her with mistrust.

The bird keeper looked at the scrawny things in open admiration.

His name was Tom, and the close-fitting green shirt and tight shorts showed off his tanned skin and toned muscles.

"Beautiful," he said, still looking at the birds.

"Beautiful," she echoed, taking in every inch of his body. She might get to like the birds.

He turned to her, a big smile showing off his perfect white teeth. All natural, she presumed. The sugar rationing for lower class people worked to their advantage.

Maud thought of the pain she had to endure to have her teeth restored to a decent shape, but she mustn't be envious. If there was one thing she believed in, it was fairness and generosity of spirit. Hadn't she given the old Annie to her gardener, and a dress to her maid? The rip in the waist could have been mended in a heartbeat.

Tom took a handful of shiny black seeds out of a bag strapped to his waist. He put his hand through the bars and whistled softly. One of the birds hopped closer on the artificial tree in the centre of the aviary. Tom whistled again. The bird hopped onto the branch nearest to Tom and pecked his finger before picking up a seed.

A drop of blood appeared on Tom's finger but he kept in smiling.

A minute or two passed. Now both birds sat on the branch, feeding.

"Let me give you some more," Maud said, brushing against Tom's bottom as she dipped her hand into the bag.

She put the seeds into his hand, careful to stay out of reach of those sharp beaks and the gnarly claws.

"Thank you." He kept his gaze firmly on the birds. Behind their tree the aviary was bisected by another bar panel, with a door inlet.

"We'll keep on feeding them like this for a bit, and then we can move into the other part until they allow us into their bit. They're pretty tame already."

He dropped the last few seeds onto the ground and pulled back his hand.

Maud touched the sore spot. "Why did they attack you?"

"It was a mistake, Miss Delancy. He didn't realise my finger was inedible."

"Call me Maud. Now that we are going to see so much of each other."

Her pendant throbbed. Pandora, doing another physical. The AI must have detected a quickening of Maud's pulse. "Get used to it," she muttered under her breath.

"Pardon?"

"I was reminding myself of a few things. Do let me know if your accommodation is satisfactory, or if you need something. Towels, pillows."

Did she detect a faint blush on those chiselled features?

She smiled to herself as she sashayed off. Tomorrow she'd wear a dress, with a good amount of cleavage.

Lunch without a glass of wine was a disappointment, but having the new face giving her smouldering looks almost made up for it. Her liver felt the benefit. Not a twinge all day, but instead all this nice frisson with the new Pandora face and the delicious Tom…

So much better after all this upheaval the day before. She detested ungratefulness, and those accusations that Rose had heaped upon her had cut her to the quick.

"Pandora, please arrange for an assortment of gardening bots to be sent to Rose, with my best compliments. Send a bottle of Champagne too, now that I can't have it."

"VERY WELL, MISTRESS MAUD."

That voice sent shivers of anticipation down her body. So velvety and dominant – "I think I shall call you Pan while we use his voice and this face. You don't mind, do you? Such an improvement over the last image."

"I SHALL REMEMBER IT."

Maud leant back in her upholstered armchair. What would life be without her trusty Pan? Bots were all very well for small tasks like serving her morning tea in bed and sweeping the floor, but Pan managed everything for her, her social calendar, her physical health, her romantic trysts when she felt so inclined – downtown was the most marvellous discreet establishment where one wore a mask and not much else.

Maud could afford to forget things because Pan did not.

Maud giggled, not her carefully modulated public trill, but a genuine giggle. To think of those misguided protesters and doubters who saw over-reliance on AI as a danger. Simpletons, the whole lot.

Nobody believed stronger in the common good and that every individual had its part to play than Maud. Did she protest when she was told of a chocolate shortage? Or when her favourite cook reached retirement age, although no one else since then came even close to producing the perfect soufflé?

Maud had borne it with grace and understanding. Just like she bore those meetings at the Ministry, when it came to working out how many children the middle class would be allowed to bear in the coming mating cycle.

The discussion tended to get heated, and for someone like Maud who considered children snotty-nosed nuisances best left to those of inferior intellect, they proved dull to the extreme. But she never shirked. Delancys always did their duty, with a smile for the official minutes.

She nibbled on her left pinkie nail.

"CAREFUL SO YOU DON'T CHIP IT AGAIN," Pan said.

"It's chipped already." He gave her a fond smile. She stopped. "Is that better, Pan?"

"YOU WILL GET USED TO THE NOT DRINKING, MISTRESS MAUD."

"What am I doing this afternoon?"

"FIVE KILOMETRES ON THE TREADMILL, TO KEEP YOUR LEGS FIRM, A SECOND FEEDING WITH THE BIRDS, AND A PUBLIC DINNER WITH AN ANNIVERSARY SCREENING OF COMMUNITY SPIRIT."

"Excellent." She could have screamed. These public dinners were the bane of her life, with the insipid wives, and men she wouldn't touch with the aid of a bot. As for Community Spirit, officially the longest running show in the world for generations, it was all very well for the lower classes, but for a person of refinement it was agony. She didn't need preaching to. She could do all the preaching herself, thank you very much.

If she survived this evening, she deserved a reward. One with a mask on.

*

Two days later, the novelty of Tom and the birds wore thin. The lack of alcohol made every fibre in her body pulsate with anger the whole time. This wasn't worth it. Nothing was worth this. Except – Maud stood naked in front of her floor-length mirror, with Pan's face watching her - the thought of another scar was hard to bear.

"There must be an easier way."

"THERE IS, MISTRESS MAUD. THE IMPLANT."

Yes. The implant. It allowed the AI to connect directly with the human brain. No need for spoken orders, and it could control cravings. It could also be removed at any time.

"How many successful trials have there been?"

"ELEVEN. NO HITCHES."

Maud nibbled on her pinkie again, until she saw Pan's reproachful look. That face! If she could have that implanted in a man, she might get married one day. But she'd have to be able to control her mate. Now that was an implant worth developing.

"No more problems?"

The idea of electronic interfaces in the nervous system wasn't new. The first generation had been tested on the lowest strata, but a spike in electrical currents had exploded that idea. Literally. Maud had seen pictures of the victims. But progress always demanded sacrifices.

"I'll think about it."

She wrapped herself in a bathrobe. Underneath her window, a spider bot happily snipped away at a hydrangea. Maud felt very pleased with herself for remembering that name. That pink was one of her favourites, except – what was the bot doing?

"Pan, what's going on in the garden? No, don't tell me, I'll go down myself."

*

Angry tears formed in her eyes. The hydrangea was a mess. Instead of being pink and the size of a melon, the flower heads looked shrunken and brown. They littered the whole ground, and the bot still snipped away, almost nipping Maud's toes in her strappy sandals.

"Stop that."

The bot turned off with a whirr.

Maud looked around. Everywhere her pleasure gardens showed signs of decay. Wilting flowers, sprouting weeds, nothing was right.

She kicked the bot. Pain shot through her toes as they hit the cold metal. Her head spun. This couldn't happen. This just couldn't happen. Not to her, of all people.

"What have the bots done, Pan? And the lawn boys?"

"WHAT THEY WERE INSTRUCTED TO DO, MISTRESS MAUD. OBVIOUSLY, THEIR INFORMATION WAS INCOMPLETE."

"I knew it. That's John's doing. He always harped on about how indispensable he was, the old fool." She kicked a dead flower head. That felt better.

"Where is he, Pan?"

"HE SHOULD STILL BE IN THE ASSESSMENT FACILITY, MISTRESS MAUD."

"Call me a glider."

*

The assessment facility reeked of disinfectant and despair. A windowless block of concrete, hidden behind metal gates in a deserted part of town, where geography had formed an anomaly so acid and radiation had taken longest to wear off.

A grey-faced gnome looked Maud over. She drew herself up as tall as she could. "Let me through," she said through clenched teeth.

He handed her an electronic tag, on a wire bracelet. "You need this."

Maud shuddered, but put the bracelet on. Honestly, the things that were demanded of her.

The gnome rang a bell. A pretty young nurse stepped lightly around the corner, a surprised look in her amber eyes. Maud disliked her at first sight. Too young, too pretty and too full of herself for her station in life.

"Yes?"

Even her voice sounded sweet.

Maud glared at her. "I am Miss Delancy, and I need to see a recent retiree. My gardener. John."

"Last name?"

"Delancy."

"I'm sorry." The nurse smiled but it didn't reach her eyes. "John's last name."

"Does he have one? Honestly, how hard can it be? John, gardener, black or rather dirty-looking, came here – I think four days ago."

"I'll check for you. If you will follow me."

The nurse led Maud down a grey, cavernous hallway. The rubbery ground squeaked under Maud's shoes.

"Here." Maud found herself in a waiting room, with scratched metal chairs and nothing else.

"Excuse me? Do you realise who I am?"

"I'm afraid this is the best we have. Unless you'd care to wait in the morgue. We've got a few beds there."

"Your sense of humour is inappropriate."

"I'm sorry. I won't be long."

Maud narrowed her eyes as she watched the nurse slip away. That girl would pay for her insolence, as soon as Maud had what she came for.

Her pendant throbbed. Her heartbeat must by now have reached critical heights. She counted backwards again. That felt better.

The nurse returned.

"If you will follow me."

She led Maud down another corridor, and made her sit down outside a big window. Behind the window was a ward, with half a dozen beds. John lay in one of them. At least she thought it was John. The face was dark enough, with even blacker bruises, and a heavy plaster cast on his arm. Tubes ran from his body to a machine next to him.

Next to him lay an old woman with a face like a shrivelled apple, talking to John.

Every single person in that room was old, useless, and unsightly.

"You don't expect me to go in there?"

"No."

"Good. Bring him out."

"I'm afraid that's not possible."

"Then how am I supposed to talk to him?"

The nurse smiled again, with a hint of insufferable smugness.

"I can act as a go between."

"Alright. Scratchpad, please?"

"Pardon?"

The nurse was obviously mentally deficient.

"I need a scratchpad to write down my questions, and you need to write down the answers."

"We don't have any spare pads I'm afraid."

"Very well." Maud snapped her bag open and took out her ruby-encrusted scratchpad.

"Careful, it's a prototype. Newest generation. Voice-operated, but only by me. I assume you own at least a stylus."

"Second generation, yes. Will that work?"

"Right. I need to know everything about plant care. What do the bots need to do? Feed, snip, water, you know all the mundane tasks. And instructions for the lawn boys. I can't have the grass wilting."

*

Bad eyes or not, John had noticed Maud as soon as she came into the fore-room. His scalp prickled when she was around, always a bad sign.

She could count herself lucky she was out of his reach, or he'd have strangled her with his one good hand. He had nothing to lose here, did he? So what did she want? Watch him die?

His neighbour prattled on. A feisty old woman, that Maizy, feisty but sweet. His wife would have liked her.

His beautiful Grace…

Nurse Janey bent over him. A nice girl, that one, always trying to make his pain go away, and to make time for a chat with him and Maizy. She was the one good thing happening to them in this vile old place.

They told him he was here to heal, and then he'd be sent to another gardening job, an easy one, but he could smell a lie a mile away. Like he could smell Maud. He'd been sent here to rot.

Nurse Janey touched his cheek, "John?"

"Yes, my lovely?"

"See that lady over there?"

"Lady?" He snorted. "Look at my face, and my arm. Her doing."

"I see. Sorry, I didn't know."

"You couldn't. Only one thing sweetheart, don't let her know your name, or Lady Muck will have you out of a job before you can spit at her. You could catch pneumonia just clapping your eyes on her."

"Thanks for the warning."

"What does she want from me?"

"Her garden's dying. She needs help."

"From me?"

A sudden warmth spread in John's battered body. He'd told her that she needed him, time and again. But she wouldn't listen. It pained him that the plants, his beautiful, much loved plants, took the rap, but he couldn't save them. Not from here.

"Tell her she needs to get me out of here. Reinstate me."

Nurse Janey looked at him with a painful tenderness.

"She can't."

"She got me here. She can get me out."

"There's too much damage, even if they would agree to make an exception."

"Damn the bitch. Damn her poxy bots."

"I'm so sorry."

"I know you are."

He lay back, his breath ragged and painful. Just for one minute he'd had hope. But now everything was slipping through his fingers again, the sunshine, his wife, the children, his flowers. He let the tears fall unhindered.

Maud was watching him, through that poxy window. He'd wipe that smirk off her face, and if it was the last thing he'd do.

He started to talk. Nurse Janey leant closer, to catch every word. She pressed a kiss onto his forehead when he was done.

*

"Well?" Maud forced herself to give John a little finger wave through the window. She snatched the scratchpad.

"There's nothing on it."

"Because he didn't say much. Mostly that he'd have to be there, in person."

"Well, he can't, can he." Maud's blood pressure rose just thinking of that rude woman at the department of labour division she'd talked to before she came here. It seemed that although Maud could send people here, once they fulfilled the age requirements, she could not have them de-admitted. She could try, of course, but it would be a lengthy process. By then, her garden would be dead.

"What did the old fool say?"

The nurse gave her a tight little smile. "He said that the plants need fertiliser, and nutrients, which he mixes according to their needs. You need soil samples from every bed, and have it analysed and the food mixed up."

"That's all?" Maud perked up.

"Almost. He said, there's one thing that matters more than most."

"Cut the drama, and spit it out. What did he say?"

"He said, you should not get your hopes up too high. Because plants thrive on love."

*

That night, Maud shut out Pan's warnings as she reached for liquid comfort. By the third glass, the memories of that stinking facility and that rotting old fool faded into a warm, fuzzy glow. Love. She could do that. Hire people to talk and sing to her flowers. Tom could do that. He whistled to the birds all the time. Cleo and Tony, he called them. Short for Cleopatra and Mark Anthony.

She refilled her glass, spilling a few drops. As if she needed him telling her that. She knew things. She knew lots of things. Nobody got the better of Maud Delancy. Nobody.

A stabbing pain made her drop her glass.

Bloody liver. These things should really last longer than a few months.

"Pan, check my vitals."

The face watched her unwaveringly as Pan bathed her in radiation.

"THE LIVER CAN STILL BE SAVED IF DRINKING IS ABSTAINED FROM FOR A PROLONGED PERIOD."

"And a transplant?"

"WOULD BE EFFICIENT FOR A MAXIMUM OF A YEAR, JUDGING BY OUR STATISTICS."

"Dammit."

She crouched as a new stab tore through her.

"That interface implant…"

"WOULD ALLOW ME TO STOP YOU FROM HARMING YOURSELF."

She whimpered.

"SHALL I SCHEDULE IT FOR TOMORROW MORNING, MISTRESS MAUD?"

She nodded, unable to speak.

*

"I want a cheese omelette, and toast."

The bot next to her bed stood still, proffering on its surface only tea and a mashed banana. Madam Whiskers rose from her cat bed in the far corner and strolled closer, radiating curiosity.

"THIS IS WHAT THE DOCTOR PRESCRIBES." Pan smiled down at her, radiating dominance and trustworthiness.

The cravings stopped. "Thank you, Pan."

"YOU'RE WELCOME, MAUD. I'LL TAKE CARE OF YOU. FROM NOW ON, I'LL TAKE CARE OF EVERYTHING."

Madam Whiskers jumped onto the bed and eyed Maud. It should have bothered her but it didn't.

She sank back into her pillows, an unknown happiness filling her heart. This was so simple. Pan would make all the decisions for her. No need to make all the decisions, all the time. She should have gotten this implant a long time ago.

Written by Rachael Howard

Hello. Where am I? Do you know where my daughter is? She told me to stay indoors. I'm not sure she'll be happy I'm here. I only wanted some fresh air. Not that you can get that these days. Not the proper stuff. This stuff they put up with these days. It's got no smell. You need a good smell, don't you? Some flowers and sweat and fresh cut grass and farts and…

Oh. You're a gardener? Lucky you. Bet you get a lungful of decent stuff don't you. Hold on. Let me sniff. Oh it's still on you, that earthiness and sweat.

No I'm not rude. Honestly. I meant that warm hard work sweat not the "haven't bathed for a week" sweat. Kids today don't know proper sweat. Not in their gyms. It's all clinical and antiseptic. You are the real thing, you are.

Where is it? I miss flowers. Real flowers. I can smell those are real. Where are they? I do love the smell of…

Where is my daughter? Have you told her where I am? She is such a worrier. Silly girl. So what if I forget a few things. Nothing wrong with that is there? Everybody forgets things sometimes. After all we are just human, aren't we?

Exactly. Everyone forgets things sometimes. You are quite right dear.

What's your name? John? I have a boyfriend with that name. But don't tell Mum. She doesn't approve. Are you my boyfriend? You look sort of like him. He's dark too. Proper dark like you. Not that mixed up colour of muddy cream.

I'm not offending you, am I? It's just we're of an age I'd say. Well within a decade or so. You remember when everyone was a different colour. Some of it natural, some of it tan and some of it dirt. Not that I'm saying you're dirty. Do you remember back then?

My daughter is going to be so angry when she finds I'm not there. I was going to go straight back in the cupboard only it is soooo boring. And I was only going to be out for a minute, as I said. I just wanted to peep outside and chat to someone. She does her best but it is nice to chat to someone different. Are you enjoying this chat? Well I am.

Anyway, I saw this young man down the road. I like young men. So I thought I would just pop out for a moment, as I said, and say hello.

Woo wasn't that exciting. Next thing I know he tells me to sit on a bench, kind young man, and he calls for his friends to pick me up. Before you know it I am in a car with two other nice young men, though they didn't seem very chatty. They told me off for being muddled. Like I can help that? I can't now can I. Though I am sure I was in school with them. I told them but they just laughed. Suppose they weren't that nice after all.

Oh dear. They promised they would tell my daughter where I am as soon as they found her. "We will have a good chat to her about you" is what they said. But they weren't nice to me really I suppose. Do you think they will tell her?

Mum will be so angry with me. No I don't mean my daughter. How old do you think I am? Cheeky. Mum would be livid if I got pregnant. What an idea. Mum says I have to keep my legs crossed. Silly that because you can't run away with your legs crossed so doesn't that make it worse?

I'm Maizy Goulden. Lazy Maizy my Mum calls me. Well why work if you don't have to? For the good of the community? Oh the community can do one. Demanding this and demanding that. Too bossy by half.

Why shush? I am NOT being disrespectful. I'm just saying what my husband always says. I am NOT a silly woman.

Oh, are they taking you away? Where are you taking him? Don't ask? How rude. Now you leave that poor man alone. Oh. You didn't have to push. Please let him stay. I don't want him to go. We're having a nice chat.

I'll see him soon? OK. Bye John. Don't struggle dear. We can carry on with our chat later. It can wait.

Oh. That wasn't necessary. Why did you have to make him sleep like that? You could have just reasoned with him. But sticking that needle in. Not nice.

Well I suppose if it is to stop him hurting himself. Just seems a bit mean to me. Tell him I'll see him soon, when he wakes up. Don't know what you are sniggering at young man. Show some respect.

Really. No manners. Poor man being treated like that.

Yes? I'm Maizy Goulden. Dominic? I've got a boyfriend with that name; a very naughty boy. Mum says he will get me into trouble. I like trouble. Is it time to go home yet? No?

Well I can follow you I suppose. I'd rather be going home, or with John. Stop wincing at that young man. There's nothing wrong with a bit of romance at any age.

This it? But there's nothing in here. No I don't like this room at all. I'm heading home.

Why must I go in? There's just a table and a couple of chairs. Not even a window. The light is too bright. The walls are too white. It hurts my eyes.

No. I've decided. I'm going home.

Why do you want to ask me questions? Questions are dangerous. Asking questions gets you disappeared, or worse. Nice questions? You're sure? Well if you give Lazy Maizy a kiss on the cheek then? Just there? Just a little peck?

Mwah! Got ya.

Don't be embarrassed. Just a little smacker on the lips. That's all. Bet you've never been kissed before.

Not proper? Way lad, are you a virgin? At your age? Don't try and suggest fantasy rubbish counts. Gross. Oh you don't use that? Good for you.

You know I could sort you out? You're just my type. Don't tell Mum though. She says I'm a bad girl. Being good is soooo boring.

No I can't calm down. My brain is buzzing. My daughter says my brain is… is…. misfiring. That's the word.

Do you know my Mum? She'd like you. You look smart and respectable. She approves of that. Doesn't approve of me though.

Where is my daughter? She should have come and collected me by now. I'd better go look for her. Stay here? No. No. I think I should leave now.

What are you calling for a nurse for? I don't need any nurse. Let me go. I don't want to be here. I want to go home. I don't want to be calmed. What do you mean, sorting my memories in order?

Backwards? I don't want to go backwards. Backwards has bad places. I don't want to go back there. So I forget some things. Can't see what the fuss is about. You are all very silly people and I have had enough. I'm off. You can go backwards if you want but I'm going home.

Not a needle, please. I'll be good. Make her go away, please. No it's not alright. Look, no nits. Don't give me an, ouch! That hurt! Mum! I want my Mum! Horrible nit nurse. Horrible, nasty.,,

****

Hello. Is it time to go home now? A chat? Oh I like chats. Who are you? Dominic. What a nice name and what do you do dear? A writer? Have I read anything of yours? Oh. Not that type of writer. Never mind. I'm sure it will happen one day.

You can't point a camera at me. Not with my hair like this. I don't even have my lippy on.

Only children seeing it? That's OK then. Hello kiddies. I'm Lazy Maizy. I like kissing boys.

What's wrong? Well they have to learn about these things someday. You can't expect them to stick to that virtual stuff. It's not natural. Kids don't go on that virtual stuff when you are older. Stick to the real stuff.

Oh alright. I'll just answer questions? If I can hold your hand? No kisses I promise. I'm ready.

My name is Lai… is Maizy. Stop frowning at me. I stopped myself didn't I?

I'm 85 years old I think. That better? Good. Because I'm not doing it again. Bad enough a lady has to reveal her age at all.

I'm not sure of my age because they don't do parties anymore. I used to like parties. All your friends would come around, real friends that is. Who you knew. In person. You're frowning again. He frowns too much, kiddies. It will give him wrinkles doing that. Don't you lot frown.

Anyway, everyone would bring you a present. Some would be big and some would be small but they were all special because your friends had chosen them for you. Themselves. Not off some approved list. Ha. Don't you dare frown at that. I want a smile. Come on. Just a little one, turn that frown upside down. Now that's better. Made you chuckle didn't I.

Look at the camera? Sorry kids. Here we go. Close your eyes and imagine it. There was lots of food and cake. You got a great big birthday cake and you could eat as much as you wanted. Really. Nobody counted it or made you pay back with stupid exercise. You could just bury your face in it like this. Mmmmmm. Bet you opened your eyes to see that, didn't you.

Not healthy? Of course it wasn't healthy. It was a party! Not healthy indeed.

Now my wedding cake. That is beautiful. Have you seen it? Four tiers. Don't want a silly three layer one. Holy Trinity my foot. Where's God now when we need him. Not even any churches.

Mum's made the outside out of cardboard. She's painted it and made it so beautiful. Of course the real cake is tiny. Hidden inside. She managed to find some real raisins to go in it though and proper sugar. Plus she got me a notepad and pencil for my stories. Haven't been able to write for years. Not approved of any more.

Someone else told me she bartered her wedding ring for them. Turns out she does love me after all. Silly that she never told me herself. She's so scared of caring and then being hurt. Because of Dad I suppose, when he disappeared.

But you have to have love in your life, haven't you? Somewhere? Or life is so miserable it's not worth living. That's what I think anyway. I will always find someone or something to love. I don't want to be like her.

Sorry? What? We can talk about that later? OK. But I will be off soon to get my hair done. I'm having it in ringlets with flowers.

Flowers? Pretty petal things. What do they do? They make things beautiful my lovely. Oh I do like flowers. They had wonderful colours and smells, so much variety. Ask that John. He knows. He's been with the real ones.

That's what this place needs, some variety. Everything is the same, the houses; the food; the work; the people. They are all the same drab colours.

We should all go around with a flower behind our ear. That would get people smiling. I do miss flowers. I called my daughter Flower.

Why's she tapping her watch? Tell her to go away.

No I didn't have someone to approve me for motherhood. I just did it. Well my husband and I just did it. She is so beautiful. Can you see those sweet curls at the back of her neck. Smell her head. That is baby smell, that is. My lovely Flower. That's what I've named her. People tell me I'm silly but that's how she makes me feel. Like I am burying my head in flowers. Only there aren't any flowers any more, not real ones. That's what they tell us but John found them, didn't he? Wonder where?

So she is my secret flower. I wish he had been here to see her. He'd have loved her you know.

Now what will I do on my own with Flower? They are telling me she should live at the school with the other kids but that's not right. Only toffs do that. Dump their kids on strangers. It is so wrong. Taking the babies away so the parents can keep working. Poor babies.

But not my Flower. She's staying with me. They say I won't last because I won't be earning money but we'll manage. I'll do anything for my Flower.

Sssshhh little one. Don't cry. Mama will keep you safe.

Lavender's blue, dilly dilly, lavender's green,

When I am king, dilly dilly, you shall be queen,

How will that be, dilly dilly, how will that be?

Because we are strong, dilly dilly, fighters are we.

Keep your voice low, dilly dilly, don't let them hear;

United we'll turn, dilly dilly, nothing to fear.

Up we will rise, dilly dilly, when all can see,

What we've endured, dilly dilly, then we'll be free.

If you should die, dilly dilly, deep in the fray,

You're name shall ring on, dilly dilly, every free day;

When shall it start, dilly dilly, when shall it start?

You'll know the time, dilly dilly, deep in your heart.

Always gets her to sleep, that one. Are you OK? Yes it is a beautiful song. I imagine you've heard it before. You have the look about you.

Bet the nurse hasn't though. She seems to have gone a funny colour. Hey, stop worrying lass. It's just a song. What danger in a song?

You know, I've been thinking. You could help me. I'd be really grateful. Very, very grateful. You don't want my little Flower to starve do you? They say she can get food if I let them put her in the school but that isn't proper. Don't know what they will be feeding her.

So lover what do you want me to do for you?

Well there's no reason to look so disgusted. I've a good body. I'm breastfeeding so the weight will go soon. Oh stop retching. It's perfectly natural. That's what boobies are for.

No. Don't edit it out. The kids need to know. They don't realise all this isn't normal. That there is better out there, somewhere. There must be. No I don't believe it is poisonous out there. Never did. Hubby told me he'd heard things. I believe what he said, not you. What rumours? Well he told me that he'd seen…

No. Not another needle, please. I'll be good. I promise.

Please, don't argue with the nurse. I shouldn't have said anything. I don't want you to get in trouble. Please stop. I don't want… I don't… bad things will happen. Please.

Thank you. Yes. I'm OK now. It is just all the stress. Flower needs weaning soon and they keep putting the price of the baby food up. I don't know how I can afford it. I don't know how anybody can afford it.

They want all the babies put in the school but I'm not going to. She is mine. She's all I've got. Except this body. What's wrong with using it to protect my baby? Better than letting them take my Flower away.

Not for long anyway. Once that credit system comes in they're talking about there'll be no spare cash for me. They'll be watching everything we spend. Then they will know. They'll stop me then. If I can just last until she is old enough to be left for a bit. She'd be safe then.

I'd make the room safe for her. I'm a good Mum. Safer in school? Never. You don't know what's going on in there. Could be anything. No. A child should be with its parents.

I'll make her a palace out of cushions and teach her not to open the door or go with the bad men if they force it open. I'll show her how to hide so they can't drag her away to the school. We'll be OK.

Could you tell your friends at least? Just on the quiet. Don't want THEM to know or they'll call me an unfit mother and take her away. She's all I've got. So beautiful. Look. Isn't she?

You want to know about my husband? They say it's an accident but I don't believe it. He'd NEVER go in the furnace until it was cold. No business being down there anyway. He should have been in the office. Someone must have sent him.

Who? I'm not saying who but someone must have. I know it.

Of course the authorities blamed him. Said he wouldn't listen and that's what happens when you don't listen to sensible advice. They had told him what to do to keep safe but he was… what did they say? That's it. They said he was emotionally and intellectually defective.

How could they say that? Of course I got no compensation, even though I had little Flower inside me.

They said it was self-inflicted. But he would have never left us. He loved us so much. I just can't believe he'd do that.

Not that I'm saying the powers did it to him, nurse. Oh no. I wouldn't dare… dream of saying something like that. You can put the needle down. "Society for us all" and all that.

Has she put it down? Oh good.

Dominic, I've been telling him those meetings will lead to trouble. They don't like you questioning things. Questions are bad. You'll see. Asking questions gets you answers and you won't like them. No way.

But he would keep asking. Why can't we go outside our level? Why can't we see a record of food distribution? Why can't we have a say in what's going on?

He got beaten up a few times, when they were breaking up the meetings. He was a good speaker you see, my hubby. People listened. It was like he glowed when he spoke. Magical.

But of course asking questions leads to trouble. They don't like you asking questions. Just do what you're told.

He said they wanted robots, not people. That we were just parts in a machine and we needed to know what the machine was really doing.

Parts in a machine. He said that a lot. Have you ever wondered about that? Why we are here? What we are doing? Is any of this –

Ouch! Bloody needles.

****

Where did I meet him? Meet who? Oh my lovely hubby? It was beautiful.

A really hot summer. More like it was scorching. They say the ozone layer is too thin or the air is bad. That we can only go out now when there is an all clear. That I risk cancer going out even then but I'm making the most of it while I can. The all clear hardly happens any more. Bigger gaps between. Wonder when it will stop for good.

My friends are saying I show too much. But how else am I to keep cool? So hot out here.

Mmmm. That breeze. Can you feel it? Undo that overall a minute. Feel the breeze on your skin. Delicious.

No, nothing like air conditioning at all. That blasts. A breeze whispers. It teases. Nothing like it. You've never felt it? How sad. Feel it now.

Ah. Look at him over there. Now that's the man I want to marry. So dark and lean. He's smiling at me.

Quick, tell me if he is still looking. Don't just look! Pretend you are looking somewhere else.

Can't see? You are useless you are.

Oh. He's spotted me looking. What a wicked grin. I'm a sucker for a grin. Has it got hotter or is it me? I need to undo a few more buttons to cool off.

What are you squawking for? I'm still decent! OK I'll do them up. He's got the message anyway. I'm going to marry him. I just know it. Don't care what Mum says.

"Men are dangerous," she says. "They make you fall in love with them then do something stupid," she says. "They put your life in danger when they risk theirs. You could get killed falling in love with a man."

Don't know why she talks like that. Dad wasn't stupid and she didn't die.

Look how he walks. That's a proper stride. All that strength in one body. Makes my heart -NOOO! Why does the alarm have to go off now. It's been hardly any time at all. I don't want to go back under ground. Seems OK to me.

Everyone is running for cover except him and me. Kindred spirits. Oh he's pretending he's a dog chasing them in. Woof. Woof. Come on. Let's chase those silly sheep. Woof. Woof.

We are the only ones left now. Look. He's nodding to the shelter. We've shown who are the wolves round here. Time to take cover I suppose.

Hope we have another safe day soon. Don't want to wait six months again. But if I'm with him I suppose I'll manage. I will be with him.

Isn't he perfect? What do you think? What do you mean does he match my breeding statistics? He's a hunk. Of course I don't need approval.

Testing? That is so gross. Are you a pervert or something? No. It's love.

Love at first sight. What else could there be. And we'll have lots of kids. They keep telling us we have to watch the population, that resources are low. But it's natural to have kids. I want lots and lots of kids. All running in and out of the house and getting into scrapes

I want to take them to the beach and the woods and up in the mountains and… But they tell us that is all gone now. We have to accept being underground.

How can kids grow up properly underground? I was always sneaking off as a kid. I loved to explore. How can they develop properly without that? What will they become? It scares me sometimes.

Am I working class? Well Mum and Dad are middle class I suppose, because of their jobs. But it is still work so I don't really understand it properly. My Dad is, was, an accountant. My Mum's a teacher. She is always teaching me. On and on and on and…

She says I should be reading more instead of sneaking off to the woods and the river. But it is lovely there. You can find all sorts of interesting plants in amongst the trees. It is so quiet. I like the quiet. You know, real quiet. No cars, no babble, no sirens. Just the hush and the odd rustle of the leaves or a scuttle in the undergrowth.

Describe it? Look it is just there. Like I'm describing to kids? They can't get out there themselves? That's horrible. They must be so poorly if they can't see it themselves. OK.

Little flowers peak out of the ground, white and yellow. Beams of light through the branches make them flash, little stars they are. I suppose that virtual stuff could give you an idea, a sense of it. But it is not really the same.

See. Insects crawl everywhere. Don't be scared. They won't hurt you.

Look. This is a woodlouse. An ancient animal. It has survived so much. It tickles. No it isn't dirty. We need them or we would be buried in rubbish. It is sweet. I'll just pop it back.

Oh yes. Well it is like...like... you know what a king crab looks like. No? You know. They look like a woodlouse but live on the shore and in the sea.

Of course things live in the sea. That is a horrible thing to say. There are fish and whales and lobsters and - OK. OK.

Well there are tall trees all around. Their trunks reach towards the sky. Describe that? Oh it is blue of course, with the odd white clouds. I love to spot what they are. From their shape. For fun of course. Pleasure. You poor boy. You have had a sad life.

So the trunks are rough and smooth. Thick and thin. Brown and silver. There is an earthy smell. I miss that smell. What is it like? Well it smells of damp and soil and... how do I explain it?

No it is NOT like that virtual stuff. People only accept that because they don't know the real thing. How can you know the thing it shows you is a tree if you've never seen the real thing. It is all a big fraud.

You don't seem to know anything. Get out there. Go see it. You need to experience life!

Oh I am bored. Can I go now? I want to go for a walk. I don't like this place. Where are the windows?

Talk about my husband? What husband? Don't be silly. I'm too young to get tied down just yet. How can I remember him if he doesn't exist?

See, like the nurse says, sort of. I can't go forward. That's time travel. Don't know what she's talking about with that silly injection though. Stop asking the poor lady silly questions. She can't reverse time. Why should she have warned you? It's obvious.

I'm going. Excuse me nurse, can you undo these straps for me please? No? What do you mean no! Undo them now. I won't calm down. Get these off me. I want to go home. Mum! Mum! Help!

What? Oh for the camera? Well I won't move if you just take these off me. Wasting time? Who's time? You're wasting my time, nurse. I want to go home!

OK. I'm doing deep breaths. Don't let go of my hands please. Yes. I'm calmer now, just while I keep hold of your hands? OK. That's better. Look. They left marks on my arms. Yes. I will be calm now. Thank you.

You are a nice man. Nice eyes too now you've taken those glasses off. Gentle eyes. Why are they so sad? You need to smile more. You must have something to smile about. Everyone needs joy in their lives.

If you have a drink of water it will stop your coughing nurse. You should know that.

Back to questions? OK. Well I am eighteen. Mum says I had to have a job. I suppose so. Gives me something to do and she needs help with the bills.

Yes it is allowed not to work. If you can afford it of course it is. Anyway who's going to stop me?

I want to write you see. I have lovely stories in my head about birds and foxes and dolphins and… They are animals. Beautiful animals. I'm told that I am good at writing stories. Making up tales. Mum says it is because I am so good at lying but I'm able to tell the truth in my stories. I can escape.

Virtual reality? Oh, only the rich have that. Most of us have to make do with the real thing. I prefer what I can really touch and smell.

The rich? Those with loads of money and land who can do what they like and have everything. No it isn't fair but Dad would say things never change. But it doesn't matter because anyone can make a nice place in their heads when they read. I make happy places for people who read my stories.

I don't understand. Why is it valueless? I make people happy. How is that not contributing? Art makes people beautiful. It makes them feel something. If people are happy then society is better, surely? It encourages people to dream of something better. To fight for something better. There's no change, no improvement without art.

There I go. Dad called it my passion. Mum says it is just me trying to get attention. But what would I do without my writing? I have to let out how I feel somehow and writing is the best way to do it. The safest way.

Who knows how I would turn out otherwise. Looking for love in all the wrong places probably. Looking for some emotion. If they stop me writing…

You write too? Tell me a story, please. Oh, that's not proper writing. That is just being a scribe. A recorder. You should write about something you are passionate about. Something that you feel a lot. What makes you want to scream out? That is what you should write about.

Mum's made me get a job. I suppose I am lucky though. It is outdoors, found it myself. Mum wanted me working with her at the school, that would have been awful. I've only just escaped.

I love my job. Helping to study the animals and plants. Watching their population and spread. Leaving traps, tagging them. I love being outside the city.

Though my boss is so sad. Like you. He says we are all doomed but the others say he is just scaremongering. Still, I haven't seen any butterflies for a while, migrating birds are fewer each year too. Probably just the weather. They'll come back.

No. Some people are told where they are working but I'm bright. I get to choose. Hate exams and stuff though. Mum says it is a waste to not do them and I should work harder but I just want to enjoy life. What's wrong with that?

Daddy understood but he isn't here anymore and Mummy says it served him right. She says I am to stop asking questions or I will disappear too. Daddy loved to answer my questions. He said it was important to think.

What's school like? Oh I hate school. You have to sit in that stuffy classroom and learn useless stuff. I like my Maths and English but I love the Biology stuff the most. Ssssh. Don't tell but I write stories in the other lessons. They get mad if they catch me. Say stories will never save the world.

But that's the grown-ups jobs. They should be saving the world, not dumping it all on us. Grown-ups are so miserable all the time.

Come on you. Laugh with me.

That was pathetic. Come on. Laugh from your belly. Let it rip. Throw your head back. Here, I'll tell you a joke. How can you tell if there are elephants in the fridge? Giant footprints in the butter. Oh my sides hurt.

You don't understand? An elephant is big, massive, with a trunk. Not a suitcase a… Oh I see. Clever one. Oooh. You smiled. Don't try and hide it. I saw it. Lovely. I'll accept a smile. A kiss would be nicer but you're a bit too old for me. Now you laugh. What did I say? Come on. Tell me.

Alright. If you won't talk.

What's all that shouting outside? I can hear screams. Someone's shouting for their Mum. Why isn't someone helping her? She sounds so upset. Should we go out and help? Poor woman. I want to go out and help. Please. Unlock the door. I want to get out there and help her.

She's banging the door. It's giving me a headache. Poor girl.

No I'm not your Mum. I'm just a girl. Please stop banging. You'll hurt yourself. I'm sorry. I'm not your Mum. Please someone out there. Find her Mum for her.

This is terrible. Why won't anyone help? No. They aren't helping. I can only hear her. It's alright. Hold on. Someone will come soon. Please stop crying. They will find your Mum soon.

Remember? Remember what? What do you want me to remember?

Come on. Open this door. If I could hug her I'm sure I could calm her down.

I can hear someone coming. Oh. Why is she screaming? No she isn't OK. Listen to her. What was that bump? She has stopped screaming now.

Is she OK do you think? Well I suppose she is in the best place to get better. Lots of nurses around. Though hopefully they aren't like you. How you could just stand there with a bloody needle in your hand while someone was clearly suffering. What are you? Some stupid jobsworth?

You should have ordered her to open that door and help. Disgraceful.

What's that? A jobsworth. Someone who only does what their job description says, takes it literally and does nothing more. What do you mean that's normal. It's not human, that's what it is. You just become parts in a machine.

Now where did I hear that said. On the tip of my tongue.

What, another question? Haven't we finished yet. I feel quite shaken up. Starting school. That was horrible. Can we have a happy question instead? I'm feeling upset enough as it is.

I don't want to go to school. Why do I have to? Mummy says the bad men will come and take me there if I don't go. I don't want to go with the bad men. I don't want to go to school. I want to be with my Mummy and Daddy but Mummy says they have to work.

The school is full of boys and girls like me. Daddy takes me to the teacher. It is all big and scary and loud but teacher is nice. Teacher gives Daddy a big hug. No I can't be at the same school as Mummy. She is with the older boys and girls. We are just little.

Teacher tells us a story every morning. I love stories. Today's one was about a scary witch who came from another country and was poisoning everything with her bad spells. So our country was really clever and made our own witch to poison their country.

Teacher said it was the right thing to do because they were bad people and were trying to hurt us so deserved it. But she looked sad when she said it.

I whispered to her that I wished there were no bad witches and no poison. I wished there were no bad things and everyone could be happy. She whispered back that she wished that too but to keep it safe inside or we would be punished. I don't want my teacher to be punished. I won't even tell Mummy and Daddy.

You won't tell anyone, will you? Please? Oh thank you.

Can we talk about something else? We can?

What makes me happy? Ooooh I know. Feeding the duckies!

Mummy says we can go to feed them today. I like the duckies. They eat a lot of bread.

Gasp. Eat them? Nooooo! Poor pretty duckies. Please don't eat the duckies.

I want my Mummy. You are nasty. Nasty man.

You promise you won't eat them? Honest? You've never eaten animals. That is good. I'm glad. Yes, only nasty people eat animals. Why eat animals. It's cruel! Mummy says I am silly but I don't want to eat pretty animals, or ugly animals. They are nice too, just not cuddly.

I am three and three quarters. I am nearly big enough to go to school.

I like cake and sandwiches and chocolate and chocolate ice-cream and my teddy Pookum and my cat Sneezes. She sneezes a lot and it is so funnyyyy!

I am going to my friend June's to play later. Mummy calls it a play date. June is my best friend and has a big garden and lots and lots of animals. I'm going to stroke her horse and play tug with her dog and her cat has just had kittens. I'm so excited.

How did she have kittens? They come out of the mummy cat's tummy silly. Why would someone tell them off? June says I can have one if Mummy and Daddy let me. Sneezy won't mind.

June is going to keep the others. Yes all of them. No I am NOT a liar. Yes she is allowed. She can keep as many as she likes because they have a big garden and a big house. June says they will help kill the rats too. I cried when she said that. I like rats but she says they are vermin. I hate that word. It's a bad word.

No the rats aren't pets. You are silly. They are wild. Lots of animals are wild. What's a licence? No. I don't have one to have Sneezy. No. They won't take her away. I won't let them. I'll hide her in my bedroom under the…

Oh. I nearly told. Anyway you are a liar. Nobody needs one of those things. My Mummy and Daddy are very clever and they would have got one if it was real. You shouldn't lie to children. It's bad. Something bad will happen to you for that.

No I won't tell you where the hiding place is. Daddy made me swear not to tell and I don't break promises. Daddy says that bad men would hurt us all if I told. He says they don't like questions and they hate if you find answers. I'm not even to tell Mummy because Mummy wouldn't understand and I am very clever, not like Mummy.

Do you think Daddy likes Mummy? They fight a lot. Mummy says shut up and Daddy says never. Then they remember me and whisper but it is loud whispers so I hear the angry noises. I hate it when Mummy and Daddy fight.

****

Where are you going? Don't leave me. What's finished? I don't want to go with the nurse. She isn't a nice nurse. Please. Take me away. Take me to my Mummy and Daddy. Pleeeeease.

Why can't he come too? I won't go without him. I won't. I don't care about the bad men. I want him. He'll tell the bad men to go away if they come. I. Will. Not. Go. I'll scream. Aaaaaagh!

You'll come with me? Will the nurse let you? See nurse. He has told you. He's coming with me.

Can I…can I hold your hand? I'm scared. Can I?

Thank you. Yes I can manage the walk. Where are we going?

I like peaceful places. Will Mummy and Daddy be there? Why are you looking at the nurse? She won't tell us. Yes? They're there? Come on then.

Oh. No. I'm not going outside. There's the bad men. I don't want to go near them.

They don't look like good men to me. I don't think they'll keep me safe at all. Can we get away from them? This way? OK.

They are following us. Quick. Run. No? Why not? I won't hurt myself silly. I can skip too. Look.

Why must I stop. A quiet place? All right. I'll be quiet. Sssshhhh.

What was that? I heard a scream. Yes I did. Someone screamed. I'm scared. Can we go back now. I don't think

Mummy and Daddy are here. This is a bad place. I want to go home. I want…

I like that song. In. Out. Deep breaths. Please sing the song. It is a nice song. Yes I know it. I don't know where but I know it. Can I sing too? Yes. We can sing while we walk. Then Mummy and Daddy will hear me coming. Won't they?

Lavender's blue, dilly dilly, lavender's green,

When I am king, dilly dilly, you shall be queen,

Will you be my king? You could wear a shiny crown and I would have one too. Oh good.

How will that be, dilly dilly, how will that be?

Because we are strong, dilly dilly, fighters are we.

Why are you crying? Yes you are. Your eyes are wet. Mummy says people sometimes cry when they are very happy. Don't cry silly. You should laugh when you are happy.

That looks silly, a smile and tears. Why are you making that funny sobby noise? Yes you are being silly.

I know. I'll make you laugh. Like my funny face? Or this one? Or this? Grrrrr. I'm scary. That's better.

We go through that door? My legs are tired. I want to sit down. Now.

No I won't get up. Not for please, not for anything.

You'll sing with me? If I stand up? OK. Help me.

If you should die, dilly dilly, deep in the fray,

You're name shall ring on, dilly dilly, every free day;

That's a nice hug. I like hugs.

When shall it start, dilly dilly, when shall it start?

You'll know the time, dilly dilly, deep in your heart.

You're squeezing too tight. You're hurting me. Don't be silly. I won't ever stop hugging you either. Hug for ever and ever.

Oh. Keep those bad men away. Please keep them away. I don't want to let go. I promised. Don't push him. You're hurting him. Bad men.

Let go. I want to be with the nice man. Help. Please make them let go. I don't want to go in that room. It smells funny.

No. You are a bad nurse. You're lying. Mummy and Daddy are not in there. That room is scary. It has nasty wires and stuff in it. I don't like it.

Wait. Nice man. Don't run away. Please. Nice man! Please come back. I'll be good. I promise. Don't leave me. Please.

I'm scared. I'm really, really scared. Please. Please.

I want my Mummy.

Mummy!

THE COLOUR OF ROSES
Written by Nick Jackson

When my cube Wordsworth wakes me at 6:00 AM, my cheeks are already wet with tears.

I notice this in the blissful seconds before the hangover uncoils itself within me. I hope I didn't make a fool of myself last night or, god forbid, break any of the rules.

Apart from the rule about not getting drunk.

Usually, I never do this; for the rules make a neat, orderly pattern of our lives, and free us from worry – the rules *work* – but, as the reflection in my shower-room mirror attests, by the puffiness around the eyes as I put on my spectacles, there are times when alcohol plugs a hole in society's order.

And there are no rules for coping with grief.

When did the crying start?

A few nights ago. But the cause goes back a week, when I interviewed the oldie. I'm a writer, you see, for *LifeStories* – a very prestigious job. I am Citizen Second Class Dominic Goodwill and the oldie was Citizen Fourth Class Maizy Goulden, and we talked, or rather I talked and she rambled on – in between bouts of singing a lullaby – and I captured the story of her life.

And then, when we were done, I walked her to the Clinic.

Lavender's blue, dilly dilly, lavender's green...

I was probably the last friendly face she saw. Mine were likely the last kind words she heard. And as I held her hand, and told her she was going to a peaceful place, I lied.

When I am king, dilly dilly, you shall be queen...

The Clinic into which she disappeared has another name among us writers: the Final Chapter. Because that's where those too ill to contribute are cured.

The Old World word for it is *euthanasia*.

The summons pops onto my work-screen as I dock my phone. I assume it's Rufus, my editor, but this name is far more important. This name is Julietta Strang.

The Editor in Chief.

Two things about Julietta: she is High Class, and feted by legislators, administrators and ministers; people who underestimate her influence do not last long at *LifeStories*. Or last long at all, so the rumours say. There are many rumours about Julietta, she attracts them like bees to honey

(I have read about bees, and I have tasted honey). We are all advised to heed the rumours, and remember them well.

But what we remember most are her clothes.

This is the second thing about Julietta. She wears *colours*.

My own attire is like everyone's attire − white, functional, comfortable − yet Julietta has earned such privileges that she is permitted choice. It's a mark of the esteem in which the Community holds her. And fears her.

"You have your assignments, and your deadlines," dressed in a rose pink trouser suit, Julietta addresses her editors as I'm shown into her office. "Run along, boys."

The men bow and depart. I've been here only twice in my five years at *LifeStories*, and both occasions gave me terrible stomach cramps. I'm feeling them now, and they don't sit well with my hangover.

With one elegant finger, she invites me to her standing desk.

"Dear heart, I've been reading your new archive. Maizy Goulden. Wife to a dissident, parent to a progeny, consort to a host of interesting characters!" She frowns. "Sounds like my mother."

I stare, slack-jawed and wide-eyed, furiously trying to think of a response.

"It's a joke, Dominic. You're allowed to laugh."

So I do: at my own awkwardness more than anything.

"What did you make of her?"

"The subject was occasionally evasive, often confused –"

"She's not the only one being evasive," Julietta smiles coyly. "Darling boy, I suspect you did not like her."

"That is… yes."

The tap-tap-tap of her fingers drumming on the desk unnerves me.

"Did she hit on you?"

The question is as unexpected as it is embarrassing. My treacherous cheeks spare my glue-gummed mouth by *not* sparing my blushes.

"Was it her age? Never judge a person by their age! Do you know how old I am?"

Even socially-awkward me knows not to answer this question.

"Your interviewee sold her own body to keep her daughter from disappearing into the system. That is one amazing woman – and you call her a fucking *subject*."

"I-I'm sorry –"

"You damn well should be. *LifeStories'* mandate is the acquisition and preservation of knowledge; for that we need the best. Anyone who doesn't fit the remit should leave."

Is she *firing* me?

"I'll redraft –"

"I had such hopes for you, Dominic."

"No. Please! One more chance!"

She's already turned away, already decided – and yet I see her pause, see her shoulders tighten, see a faint glimmer of hope…

Julietta holds up a magnetic strip, bearing a name, barcode and face. "Tomorrow I have an engagement on the surface; another of Maud Delancy's soirees. If, by the time I return, I am not reading your new, much improved archive, I will be reading your resignation letter. Are we clear, darling heart?"

I nod, bow, take the strip and thank her for this reprieve.

As I leave her office, I run straight to the nearest toilet.

For the second time that day I'm gazing at the vibrancy of roses – only this time it comes from real roses.

There are three retirement villages within my district, but this is the best. This has underground gardens to enjoy. This has roses.

"Never thought I'd feel grass under my feet again," the old man marvels. "I'd forgotten how it tickles!"

He is Citizen Third Class Jeff Young, and has earned enough merits to be assigned to the best retirement village.

"But if there's one thing I miss more than grass under my feet, son, it's clouds over my head. Beautiful white clouds."

Jeff has worked hard for these privileges: over 70 years as an air-ventilation engineer, maintaining five allotted miles of ducting.

"Back before the Change, those were hot days, when you barely had the energy to walk. I told you about the icebergs melting, didn't I, son? Well, everything felt so slow and tired, like time had stopped. But there were always clouds, drifting by, reminding us that life went on."

An orderly brings refreshment. He pours two glasses of water and leaves them on our table beside a vase of hybrid rainbow roses.

We talk more about Jeff's memories of the surface. It sounded such a terrible time then, nations warring over trivial matters whilst people starved and crops failed and the air became heavier and hotter… and yet, when he speaks I detect a wistful longing.

And then he says a curious thing: "Y'know, the water tastes so much better up here."

Up here? We're on the lowest level.

"Guessing it's to do with how many times it's been recycled on its way down. Water don't flow upwards now, does it?"

He laughs at this. I frown.

"On it's way down *where*?"

"The Lower Levels." He seems surprised I should ask. Remembering how Maizy regressed mentally the more we talked, I credit this foolishness to old age.

Except, Jeff's watching me like *I'm* the fool.

"How many people you interviewed, son? Ballpark figure."

"What's a ballpark?"

"Tell me how many an' I'll tell you about ballparks."

"I'd guess 800."

Jeff whistles. "You met any others who done my job?"

"Lots! Probably one in 20."

"Whew, that *is* a lot."

"So, about these ballparks?"

"That's a place we used to play sports. I was always good at sports as a boy. We played a game called baseball. Man, I hit so many home-runs…" he laughs at my puzzlement. "You've no idea what I'm talking about! Bet you don't know about the World Series neither?"

"I'd like to hear about that some time."

"Deal." He basks in the warmth of treasured memories, but his smile fades when he remembers something else. Something not so pleasant. "I never did get to play catch with Ayeisha…"

I'm not expecting this. Jeff's record made no mention of a daughter, assuming that's who he's referring to. Part of me doesn't want to upset him, but he did raise the subject… And it will look good in my archive.

"Your daughter?"

He nods. "How old are you, son?"

"Thirty-one."

"You're about her age. She was mixed-race, like her momma, and as beautiful. We only had her for a year."

"I'm sorry –"

"She didn't die!" He pats my shoulder, aware of my discomfort. "She were taken. Given to another family. A *better* family, we were promised – though years later I heard lots of kids were packed off to boarding schools instead. Some even ended up in orphanages."

"*Orphanages*?"

"You heard right. Can you imagine being told your ma and pa were dead, when that ain't so?"

"Did you try to find her? Any parent..." I wince at my own thoughtlessness, but Jeff just nods.

"I only found out recently. Sure, I made enquiries... No records exist, so I were told. I'm just glad my Lucille, God rest her soul, never knew. Even though we never got permission, she *so* wanted a baby."

Jeff's eyes drift over the lawn, possibly imagining his wife there, with their daughter. "I can still hear her, singing our beautiful child to sleep."

"I wish you could have taken her to the ballpark."

He smiles, grateful. We watch a gardener wheeling a barrow filled with green and white sacks. Fertiliser, for the glass houses.

"I hear that stuff's the real deal," Jeff perks up. "Comes from *animals*!"

"What I would give to see one of those."

"Say, how big is this level we're on, son?"

"Approximately 40 miles. Same with the level above." I bite my tongue before saying the level above *that* is the surface, because Jeff thinks it's uninhabitable (and of course there's a rule about not telling them, for their own benefit). "Why do you ask?"

"I was good with the old bat and ball, but not so hot up here, y'know?" He taps his head. "Numbers especially used to throw me. Take those figures you gave – 800 interviews, and around one in 20 did my job – which I'd put at 40, but that can't be right."

"That is right –"

"That *can't* be right, 'cause we were all assigned our five miles of ducting, and if that *were* right then we'd be talking *200 miles* of ventilation for two levels totalling 80 miles."

I stare at him, speechless.

"And that," Jeff grins, "is a home-run!"

I've walked every corridor, ridden every elevator, and I know there aren't any levels below us: because there aren't any ways to *access* levels below us.

But I also know Jeff's sums are correct.

"Wordsworth, review my archives for air-ventilation engineers," I pace back and forth in my apartment. "Search for the amount of ducting assigned, where specified."

"OF COURSE, SIR," my cube's voice is well-mannered and aloof – because it's assumed writers want for a personal assistant an impeccably mannered talking dictionary – "YOU HAVE 42 ENTRIES MATCHING THAT CATEGORY, AND THEY ALL LIST THE ALLOTTED DUCTING AREA AS FIVE MILES."

"That's... 210 miles of ducting." How can this be? "Wordsworth, what's the combined area of both underground levels?"

"THIS AND THE FIRST LEVEL TOTAL 83.25 MILES, SIR."

All 42 of my engineers retired in the last five years, following a lifetime's service: meaning they were all working at the same time.

"How is it possible to fit 210 miles of ducting into 83.25 miles of underground city?"

"YOU HAVE NOT INCLUDED ARCHIVES WRITTEN BY *OTHERS*, SIR."

I stop pacing. This means there are even *more*.

"How many, Wordsworth? Confine your search to the last five years."

"INCLUDING YOURS, THERE ARE 311 REPORTS, SIR. AND THEY ALL STIPULATE FIVE MILES."

I sink onto my bed. In the last five years, 311 engineers retired from maintaining their own five miles of ducting, which comes to…

"A TOTAL OF 1,555 MILES OF DUCTING. SIR."

The elevators all look the same: a single sliding door, a large display screen for the three floors (2, 1 or Surface), and below that a raised circular button, with the arrow pointing up, down, or both, depending on the floor it's on. There are no key holes or lockpads to access hidden levels.

("A TOTAL OF 1,555 MILES OF DUCTING…")

I need a drink.

In seconds I'm heading towards the bar I swore that very morning I'd never enter again. I've got my career-saving report to write, but first I need one drink to settle me down, Then I can forget this stupid nonsense.

Three drinks later I still haven't forgotten this stupid nonsense.

Soft music plays. Subdued lighting makes this bar a favourite among those on actual dates (I've tried a few, but I didn't enjoy it. Too many variables, unknowns, mistakes waiting to be made. I don't understand the rules, so whenever I come here I come alone). This is also *the* place if you want to exceed your alcohol limit. I've been told something in the walls tricks your wrist-pad into not recognising what you're drinking. I've heard of other establishments, called Romance Palaces, which also have no limits to what you can consume. Of course I've also heard the Civil Compliance use these places to eavesdrop on loosened tongues, but that's so crazy it's worthy of Maizy…

Keep your voice low, dilly dilly, don't let them hear...

I shake my head, as though to dislodge those words from my mind. It's just a silly lullaby, sung by a mad old woman, and yet it disturbs me so.

United we'll turn, dilly dilly, nothing to fear...

The music changes. A faster tempo should drown out Maizy's haunting song. And better still, it gets louder as the bartender twists a volume dial. I raise my glass –

Wait a minute… that dial looks like –

I run from the bar.

I take the elevator to the lowest floor, wait for it to empty, wait for me to be alone, wait for the doors to close...

I reach for the raised button with the arrow now pointing upwards. My hand trembles as I try twisting it.

It doesn't move.

There are *no* other floors. I need to stop procrastinating, and write –

The circular button has a rounded edge, allowing my fingers to gain a slight purchase. Enough to pull, and… The button pops forward. As I try to move it a second time, it twists – like a volume control dial – turning a full 180 degrees.

Until the arrow button is pointing down.

Suddenly the display screen shows almost 200 new floors!

I've found the Lower Levels.

I choose a floor at random. With no idea what's down here, whatever choice I make is a guess. The door slides open. And I see –

A familiar corridor. A travelator. People.

What did I expect: aliens?

And yet... I see it in the way they walk with their heads bowed, the way they slouch on the moving pathways, the way they look so downcast. So beaten. They've spent their entire lives here, and not once felt the sun.

There *is* an alien, but it is not these poor wretches. This is their world, and I am the intruder.

Perhaps I'm imagining it, but I don't feel safe. I retrace my steps. By the time my elevator comes into view I'm running, and I throw myself inside, twist the button and stab at my floor number.

And tremble like a frightened child s the elevator ascends.

At work the following day, another summons awaits. This one is not a surprise: Rufus.

My editor's office has a traditional, sit-down desk, which he does not invite me to sit down at. From his chair behind it, he glares at me

"Are you *stupid*, Domo?"

Having written and submitted my report during the night, I've rehearsed what to say. "I doubted their existence too! But Jeff is *right*, and I can show –"

"I knew it was a mistake letting you interview a dirt-dweller."

"A what?"

He looks at me like I'm an imbecile, before calling up a holo-copy of my report. It hovers over his desk, pale green and vulnerable. In one fist Rufus crushes the image, destroys the data, and throws it away.

"We do not speak of this, Domo," he snarls. "Ever again."

The bastard. The utter bastard.

Yes, I'm back in the bar. Yes, I'm drinking. And yes, I don't give a damn about consumption rules, or tomorrow's hangover, or whether Julietta makes good on her threat to fire me; and I am getting drunk – scratch that: I'm *already* drunk – and probably already fired.

When Rufus destroyed my work, I lost it (*"I stayed up all bloody night writing that"*) made a scene in front of everyone (*silent, standing, staring at me*) and had to be escorted out (*hands grabbing my arms, dragging me away*) – and the worst thing is (*at the far end of the floor, her door opening*) she saw it all (*her dress, red like a rose, red like my rage*). Julietta watched my unravelling, my shame, and I knew my career was dead.

So, I'm back in the bar, and I'm drunk, and I want to kill my utter bastard editor.

My phone keeps vibrating. Wordsworth, probably telling me I have a fine for leaving work early; but I don't care, because…

Because…

(*"I* knew *it was a mistake letting you interview a dirt-dweller…"*)

He *knew*? Rufus knew about the Lower Levels! And if he knows, then how many others know? How many have kept the secret – and kept those people trapped below, fed lies that the surface is uninhabitable, whilst taking their…

Taking their children.

(*"I heard lots of kids were packed off to boarding schools instead. Some even ended up in orphanages…"*)

Jeff may have been wrong about the surface, but not the orphanages. I was *raised* in one.

(*"I can still hear her, singing our beautiful child to sleep…"*)

My breathing quickens. My pulse, my heart, race to see who can send me dizzy first.

Up we will rise, dilly dilly, when all can see...

It's a different voice now, a different person – please *no!* – but it comes to me, and I cannot stop it, and suddenly I'm overwhelmed by the fractured memories of a child too young to understand, of a woman screaming (*hands grabbing her arms, dragging her away*), of a mother being separated from…

What we've endured, dilly dilly –

…from her son.

– then we'll be free.

Her son. My mother.

I hardly realise the glass exploding against the wall came from my hand until, for the second time that day, I'm the centre of everyone's attention.

I don't wait around to be dragged out.

Maybe it was the drink; maybe I was afraid to go home in case the Civil Compliance know about my vandalism; maybe I thought in my drunken stupor I could actually find my mother – whatever the reason, as soon as I stumble into an elevator I choose the Lower Levels.

The journey takes longer. I've gone deeper than the previous day. How deep I do not know, until the doors open.

Until I set upon a course of action that will shatter my life.

The corridor is darker than any I've seen before. There are no people, no travelators. Instinctively I know that very few come here.

Around the corner there's a vehicle that looks like a platform on wheels, with a place at the front for a driver to steer with a joystick. Stacked on it are dozens of bags, which I recognise by their green and white colour. Fertiliser bags.

(*"I hear that stuff's the real deal... Comes from animals!"*)

This is where it's made! Already I'm feeling foolish for not going home, and even through the alcoholic haze I know I won't find my mother; but a chance to see a *real* animal…

I open the nearby door. Nobody about. I hear voices, but too far away to make out words. I choose the corridor leading towards the voices. After all, the animals can't fill the sacks themselves.

A strange sensation as I walk: the ground is vibrating.

I reach a corridor with windows looking out over a huge factory floor. The vibrations become clear: at one end gigantic rollers crush the fertiliser, then it passes along numerous conveyor belts, until it's ready for the teams of workers to shovel it into bags.

Now I can make out words: "Another batch has come down..."

I'm so close. *Real* animals! I've viewed pictures, but to see an actual cow or horse...

"Make sure you get all the rings..."

A door, ahead. It slides open, granting admittance to a gantry overlooking another factory space. I slip inside. The voices are directly below.

"You'd think the crushers would destroy 'em, but they still get through..."

Six conveyor belts rise from the lower floor, disappearing through holes in the far wall, behind which comes that loud grinding.

And then I peer over the railing.

Two men heave a large black bag onto a table before a conveyor belt. There are another five like it, all with identical bags in place, and by the wall there are dozens more black bags, waiting their turn.

Where are the animals?

Then one of the men unzips the bag.

And I see my first human corpse.

"Don't assume these oldies have already had their jewellery removed…"

A naked man lies on the rollers, feet pointing towards the inclined conveyor belt. His skin is alabaster white, as though the colour was drained along with his life. His eyes are open, staring – seeing nothing – but staring at me.

The fertiliser certainly comes from *animals*.

I gasp in horror.

And the men below hear me.

I'm running before the alarm screeches through the air.

I run through the corridors; I run past the platform vehicle; I run faster than I ever have on a treadmill, and somehow I actually reach the elevator. Then my luck runs out.

I stab the call button, but the door doesn't open. I beat on it, but still the door does not open. The indicator shows the elevator descending, but it's taking too long, and already I hear running behind me…

The door opens. I throw myself inside – to discover it's *not* empty.

A crack over the back of my head, and I'm out before I hit the floor.

I wake in a tiny, dark room. It feels as though we're much deeper in the earth, with above us hundreds of feet of concrete and soil. It feels as though I'm buried alive.

"Good, you're awake." A reedy voice behind me, to my left.

I try to turn, but my head is fixed to some kind of frame. Attempting to move only highlights the chains binding my wrists to a chair.

"Your name is Dominic Goodwill, correct?"

"What do you want?"

"I want you to answer my questions. Your name is Dominic Goodwill, is that correct?"

"You have no –"

The punch comes from my right, smashing into my shoulder and shuddering down my arm.

"Y-yes. Yes!"

"You were outside your permitted zones today, weren't you, Mr Goodwill? And not just today either."

"I don't know what –"

Another cannon-ball punch to my shoulder. I cry out.

An object is dangled in front of me. My wrist-pad. "Try again, Mr Goodwill."

"I'd… heard stories…"

"You like stories, do you? But of course, you're a *writer*."

"I won't tell anyone –"

"You'll tell me everything, Mr Goodwill."

"Y-yes."

"You heard stories. Of secret sub-levels. So decided to investigate. Correct?"

"Yes."

"And from whom did you hear these *fascinating* stories?"

I almost say his name, almost betray Jeff. But I will not do that. "I overheard it in … a bar."

The blow dislocates my arm. The room fills with an unearthly wailing that I dimly realise is me. I almost pass out – and wish I could, to spare me the pain – but these people are experts at ensuring we are spared no pain.

"We know you interviewed a man yesterday. Jeffrey Young. We also know he used to live down here. Sadly your foolish editor destroyed your work before we read it, so we do not know if he's the one who told you."

"N-n-no."

"Are you sure?"

"I-I-If…"

"Speak up now, Mr Goodwill."

"If you should die, d-d-dilly dilly, deep in… the fray,"

"Are you *mocking* me?"

"Your name shall… shall ring on, dilly dilly –"

My spectacles are ripped from my face, crushed before my eyes..

"*– every free day!*"

I laugh, my body shaking even more. There's nothing funny about this, and I'm under no illusions I will survive, but my last little act of defiance is all I have left. That, and the name I will not surrender.

"As you wish. Leave his hands and his face."

The screaming only stops when my throat is too hoarse to make a sound.

The thing that wakes on the floor of my apartment some time later, that crawls to the shower-room and hauls itself up before the mirror, that thing resembles me. My reflection is the same man – but he's not the same on the inside. He's broken and bruised and beaten down on the inside; he's cowed.

And he needs help.

"Dominic Goodwill, Citizen Second Class," the hospital's receptionist states. "You have been assigned a practitioner appropriate to your medical cover. Be seated and you will be seen shortly."

Shortly never means what it says.

My traitorous wrist-pad issues warnings from Wordsworth that I must not miss my morning exercise or be late for work – like I'm in a fit state for either. The only calories I'll shift today are from shivering; and as for my job…

My job. How I'd thought I was so important! But what am I, really? I'd ridiculed Maizy because she wanted to write stories – *"their contribution to society is valueless"* – but at least she'd wanted people to be happy. She'd wanted people to feel something, anything; she'd wanted people to dream of something better, to fight for something better – and I, the man who didn't even notice his own words revealing too many air ducts, I'd *mocked* her for it.

I'm so sorry, Maizy Goulden. I let you down.

"You are a nice man. Nice eyes too. Gentle eyes. Why are they so sad?" My eyes are swollen and blackened, but it's that sweet lady's voice in my head that brings the tears to my cheeks.

When it's my turn I'm helped into a consultation pod. The woman who examines me looks exhausted.

"You qualify for these," the doctor hands me a prescription. "Take one 30 minutes before your shift to ensure pain-free productivity." She pauses. "Relatively pain-free."

Despair tramples me. It's not enough, but my medical cover doesn't buy that level of humanity. "Isn't there… anything…?"

The corners of her mouth twitch. Does she want to help? Her intercom beeps. She picks up the handset, listens. And then she asks if I'd like a glass of water, before leaving the consultation pod.

Alone, I close my eyes from the stinging brightness of the room; the one pain I have some control over.

I hear the door open. The clink of a glass on the desk. I open my eyes, and they focus on the large pill bottle beside the water. Without glasses I cannot read the label, but I'm certain these are stronger.

As a surge of gratitude floods through me, the woman speaks.

It's not the doctor.

"Darling heart, you look *dreadful*."

Julietta is wearing orchid black. She gives me a smile as she perches on the desk.

"You… *you've* paid…?"

"Don't be silly. You've been promoted, dear one!" Julietta pats my hand. "Or at least you will be after our chat. Let's consider it your yearly review."

Like a wounded creature my hand crawls towards the pills. She rolls them away.

"It hurts…"

"And it hurts *me* to see you this way. You know, I'm acquainted with a most *excellent* doctor. He could have you up and running in no time! Just be careful he doesn't seduce you." She leans forward, as though sharing a secret. "I think he rather fancies me. Fancies himself too. Though with good reason, fair's fair."

"Please…"

"Why were you down in the Lower Levels?"

"You… know…?

"I know many things. But, once you understand, once I've impressed upon you certain truths – and you've impressed me with the appropriate response – then Citizen *First* Class Dominic Goodwill will get his medication and go home."

"Those… people… think the surface… uninhabitable…"

"An unpleasant deception. But a necessary one."

"There are… thousands."

"No, there are *millions*. And imagine what they would do if allowed up to the surface. They'd ruin it for all of us."

"People aren't… like that!"

"Are you so naïve? I credited you with a good brain, Dominic, but either I am wrong or you're concussed – and I'm never wrong. Have you forgotten those archives telling horror stories from before the Change? The wars. The pollution. The pandemics. Stories *you* wrote. But those people are safe now down below. And we are safe up here."

"The children? Why… take…?"

Julietta studies me. Decides. "A matter of population control."

She says it so calmly, like suppressing an entire people carries the same weight as ordering lunch. "We preferred to take them in the first few months. Kinder for the child."

"And… they *let* you…!"

"They'd been *incentivised* not to breed. And those who did were further incentivised to hand over the child. Those who did not soon learned that what we give, we can take away." Julietta picks up my water, takes a sip. "Some still resisted. Your Maizy was one. I do *admire* that tenacity! If only she could have been *better*."

"Better?"

"More suitable, then. For life, with us."

"You're… keeping them prisoner… letting them… die out."

Julietta laughs. "You're so melodramatic! If we wanted them dead, we'd switch off the air ventilation. We're not *monsters*, Dominic. And there are still people who don't belong with them, who belong with us! And *you* have so much to contribute." She gives me such a smile. I want to punch her face in.

"And the rest, you just… turn into fertiliser!"

"Do you know what we did with the dead before the Change? We put them in boxes, and buried them in the earth. Not good for the environment. Or we burned them, and added to the air pollution." She takes another sip. "But if you can tell me why recycling their nutrients today and creating plant life from it is a *bad* thing, I'll certainly pass your message on."

I can't think of an answer. "What I don't understand… why let me… talk to them?"

"Rufus was against it, said you weren't ready for the truth, but he's *so* boring." Julietta examines her nails. "I know you'll come round, when you understand. And then you can help."

A fresh wave of agony crashes through my body. I need those pills; but she still keeps them out of reach. "Help how?"

"We require their memories, their experiences, of the world before the Change. They can tell us –"

She stops. Smiles, aware she almost said too much.

"All in good time, darling heart."

My audacity at the scale of this deception manifests an anger I never thought myself capable of. I bite it down. "Did you… have this… done to me?"

A flash of surprise. Interestingly, she's not offended by my accusation

"Did I do what? Have you beaten almost to death? Or ask that your hands be spared?" She rises from the desk "You have no idea what it takes to ensure our survival. I hope you'll learn."

She holds out the pills. I get to my feet, unsteady but able to stand. I look at the medication, the salvation from this agony.

And I turn my back on Julietta, and I limp away.

The retirement village is quiet. Many of the patrons are on the lawn, but the one I'm looking for isn't there.

I came straight over, after claiming my prescription. When the pharmacist confirmed my allotted ten tablets couldn't cause an overdose I swallowed the lot. I don't want Jeff to see me in pain. He's suffered enough.

I check his room. I check the communal areas, the gardens, even the bathing area. But still I cannot find him.

There is only one place I haven't searched. The Clinic.

It contains three people. There's a woman, and if I allowed myself to think about it she'd remind me of Maizy. There's a man, his skin a deathly grey. And there is Jeff.

He's laid on a bed, intravenous drips pumping his body full of suppressants whilst drawing his life. Only when I rip the tubes from his arms does he wake, with a confused expression that slowly clears.

"Son… what're you doing here?"

"Trying to save you!"

Jeff shakes his head. He looks like he could fall asleep any second, and if he does I'm not sure he'll wake up again.

"Too… late." His eyelids flutter, close. I shake him. No response.

"Like hell I'm too late. You owe me another conversation, Mr Young. You never told me about the World Series!"

This does the trick. His eyes reopen, their gaze a little stronger.

It takes several moments to find the wheelchair. Manoeuvring Jeff into it isn't easy, but soon we're on our way. Thankfully the motorised chair does the work, allowing me to use it as a rest. All I need do is steer.

In the elevator I remember something.

"You need this. It'll protect your eyes as you adjust." Carefully I slide the visor over his brow. "Luckily today's forecast is a good one." Jeff looks puzzled. But before he can speak, the elevator door opens.

Onto the surface.

There aren't too many people about at this time. It's mid-morning as I guide Jeff's chair across the atrium, and soon we're in a park. He hasn't spoken so far, but he keeps looking everywhere, at the trees and the hills and the far away mountains, perhaps comparing them to memories he's cherished all his life.

And most of all, he keeps looking up.

I stop on a low hill. I lock the brakes.

Hands trembling, Jeff removes the visor. He squints, but nods to my unspoken question. And he looks up again.

"Clouds… there're still clouds." He smiles, and a tear rolls down his face. "Help me outta this chair, son, please."

With my one good arm I help him stand. He's barefoot, so as he shuffles forward the grass tickles his feet. He laughs like a boy. He tires almost immediately, so we sit on the grass, in the sun.

Jeff looks much frailer than he did just two days ago. He doesn't have much time left, not after being in the Clinic. If only I'd acted sooner.

"I'm sorry you never got to see this before."

"Son, it ain't your fault. We have no say over the times we're born into." Jeff takes a deep lungful of real air, which thankfully does not have the acrid taste of less clear days. "But it's what we do to change things that give us a voice. And the more we don't like something, the louder we shout."

"So many people I didn't help –"

"But now you have, and now there's so many more you *will* help."

I think of Maizy, and smile. "How can you tell if there are elephants in your fridge?" Jeff shakes his head at my question. "Bloody big footprints in the butter!"

The old man snorts, then chuckles, then lets out a proper, long laugh. And I tell him about the woman who told me that joke, the most amazing woman I ever met.

Time passes, as shadows move across the earth, as clouds drift across the sky, and we talk – of baseball and the World Series; of how things were and may be again; of warm sunlight on your face, and cool grass between your fingers; of growing up with a mom and dad, and growing up with nobody – we talk about so many things, but all too soon time passes.

Jeff lies back. He says it's a better view of his beloved clouds, but we both know he's fading. For him, too much time has passed.

"Ain't you gonna get into trouble for bringing me here, son?"

"I'm in enough trouble already," I smile, cough, hide the grimace. The painkillers are wearing off.

"What happened to your specs?"

"I… lost them."

Jeff nods. "Did they hurt you?"

I think back to the beating, blow after blow raining down. Inside the pain is nullified, temporarily; but later there will be a cost. What is that though to a lifetime without sun?

"I'll be fine," I lie.

We watch a large cloud shadow steadily approach. The midday heat is stifling, so its temporary shade will be welcome. I feel Jeff's hand on my arm.

"Do something… for me… will ya?"

"Anything."

"Fight them. Fight the bastards... And bring 'em crashing down."

"It will be my pleasure, sir."

And we look at each other, and we smile, and we laugh. The cloud reaches us.

"Thank you, son. For this. Your momma would be proud of you."

My eyes water, and at first I try to hold them back but then I let them go, for tears must not be bound by silly rules.

When the cloud passes on, when the grass glows again, I am alone.

I said there would be a cost.

I returned Jeff's body to the Clinic. Nobody questioned what I'd done, but when there are rules for everything, perhaps they assumed I was following orders. I don't know;

I don't care. My gamble in taking all the pills paid off, but at a price – and now it's time to pay.

I reach my apartment before the dizziness starts. It's manageable if I stay seated, so I dock my phone, increase the text size to compensate for my weaker eyes, and write the two best reports of my life. Jeff's and Maizy's stories – ones finally befitting such great people. It no longer matters if I admit Jeff told me about the Lower Levels – where he is now he cannot be harmed – but this apparent betrayal may convince others.

I have never been so focused. I have to be, for the pain is growing. And growing.

And I have nothing left to fight it with. Nothing but my words.

My final journey is agony. I can barely stand, let alone walk. The travelators take me most of the way, but not all. I won't stop though; I dare not. There's something wrong inside me, I can feel it. And for the last hour, I've been coughing up blood. The cost was higher than I imagined.

When I stagger into *LifeStories* my legs are near to collapse, my right arm a dead weight. I make it to my floor, but I am spent. The debt must be paid – and I have nothing left to give, except my life.

The room is spinning. I sense people rising from desks, but their faces are a blur. With my final drop of strength I hold out the memory stick containing archives that are too important to send electronically; and just before I lose my sight I *think* I see pink or yellow or red – my salvation, in the colour of roses – and then I'm toppling forward, hitting the floor, spasming.

Then nothing.

"Open your left eye. Follow the light. That's very good. Now the right one."

The room is strange. It looks like a doctor's surgery, yet has none of the starchiness. There are exotic plants, and one wall is a huge water tank with things moving inside.

It dawns on me that for the first time I am looking at real fish.

I've heard about them, read about them, written about them, but to *see* them…

"Those are fish," I say, pointlessly.

The man with the torch laughs. "That's the second time you've told me. The first time you were pounding on the glass. I had to sedate you."

This is news to me. "Why?"

"You were frightening the fish. They're tropical, and *very* expensive."

"No, why was I hitting the glass?"

"A reaction to the drugs I had to give you. Which reacted to the drugs you'd given yourself. Which *could* have some interesting recreational uses, once I work out a safe dosage." He has an easy smile, though whether it's friendly I cannot tell. He's the handsome confident type, who makes other men nervous. "You're welcome, by the way."

I digest these words. "You saved my life?"

"Now you've got it."

I touch my right shoulder. No pain. I can raise the arm again too. "I reset it," the man says. "And fixed the broken ribs. And the internal bleeding. And, well… what can I say? I'm a genius."

I manage a stunned thank-you. It seems woefully inadequate.

He nods. "I'd say don't mention it, but I'd much prefer if you do – to all your rich friends. Especially the pretty ones."

"You've got me confused with someone else if you think I'm rich –"

"Of course you are, Dominic Goodwill," he enjoys my surprise. "Citizen First Class."

"*First...?*" Then it becomes clear. I'd gambled on Julietta leaving her offer of 'promotion' open, and it paid off. Would I still be alive if it hadn't?

He holds his hand out. "Lucas Spiller. Doctor Lucas Spiller."

"Pleased to meet you."

"Most people are," Lucas says. "You're one of Julietta's people. Are you a lover or a writer?" My shocked expression is met with more laughter. "Just playing with you! But she is a fascinating woman, don't you think?"

I remember my last conversation with her. "You're the doctor she knows."

Lucas seems to stand a little taller. "She only picks the best. Julietta and I are alike, in many ways. I see myself in her... in many more ways." He winks. "Don't tell anyone I said that."

He busies himself putting away medical implements. I realise then he has no assistants. "You work alone?"

"Apart from a Florence, yes. This way I'm not let down by others. It's how I survive."

Carefully I lower myself from the couch, wondering how my legs will react. The dizziness, the pain, it's all gone.

"Let me give you some free advice," Lucas finishes tidying away, "next time you think about wandering around places where you're not meant to be – think again."

"You know about the Lower Levels?"

"Of course I know! A lot of the downies are my patients. Those with rich sponsors, anyway."

"Doesn't it bother you? All those people down there?"

"People have to live somewhere."

"That's not living. Parents who haven't seen their kids in years!" A strange look crosses the doctor's face. "And what else I learned –"

"Almost got you killed." I've touched a nerve, though I'm not sure what. "My day-to-day duties normally find me in less *enjoyable* surroundings. I'm usually cutting people up, not putting them back together. So listen. Knowledge is dangerous, Dominic. Never find a cause worth dying for. It's bad for your health."

"More free advice?"

"It's how you'll survive."

I'm disappointed he doesn't care that so many live beneath our feet, trapped by lies, but there will be others who do. And they will know how to use what I'll uncover at *LifeStories*. Lucas is right about one thing: knowledge *is* dangerous. And my job is all about gathering knowledge.

And not just that. Ayeisha is out there somewhere. Possibly my mother too. And Maizy's daughter, Flower – what did Julietta call her? A progeny? She could be useful…

"Wait."

I stop at the door, hopeful Lucas has had a change of heart. No such luck. Instead he hands me a small metal cylinder. "It's from Julietta," he explains.

Inside are the most expensive spectacles I've ever seen. They slide perfectly into place.

"If you get bored running blood tests, doctor, I have an alternative. The fertiliser from these plants." My turn to I wink. "Don't tell anyone *I* said that."

Lucas still has that easy smile, but I can tell he's thinking furiously. I don't know if he and I will meet again, let alone be friends, but I know I can trust him. That's how we'll *both* survive.

"What did you do to earn those?" Lucas asks, with a hint of respect.

A smile crosses my face "I hit a home-run."

Time to leave. I have much to do. I'm a writer, and I'll dream of something better. And I'll fight for something better. And my voice will be heard on every level of this hidden city. I am Citizen First Class Dominic Goodwill.

And I am free.

PATIENT #402

Written by Fiona Leitch

She shuffled through the neon-lit streets, just another hunched figure returning home after a long day at work.

The streets around the food factory were of a better class than the neighbourhood where she lived, but she still preferred the dark, over-crowded huddle of apartment blocks she called home. The people were friendlier; families looked out for one another. No one had much, but what they did have, they shared. It wasn't that they were free – she didn't believe that anyone was free, rich or poor – more that they had little to lose.

She cut through a back street, in and out of the shadowy corners that the streetlights never managed to illuminate. There were parts of the world where it was forever night, away from the 'sun' that she'd heard stories about, and those parts were the realm of the poor.

There was no crime down here – no real envy between the haves and the have-nots – it was just the way life was.

The occasional opportunistic thief was dealt with swiftly and harshly, with no right of appeal, and it didn't take long for the message to get through: Do what you're told and be grateful that the State is here to look after you.

She reached home, a high-rise block of family apartments. Breeding was the one thing that the State still let you do on your own, but it had to be approved first. More babies meant more workers for the factories.

"I'm back!" she called.

"WELCOME HOME, LOUISA." The family's AI, an Adam unit, was always polite. Not like the supervisors at the food factory. "JENNIFER IS DOING HOMEWORK IN HER ROOM. HARRY HAS LEFT WORK AND WILL BE HOME IN APPROXIMATELY 10 MINUTES."

She headed for her daughter's bedroom, pausing in the doorway for a moment to watch her beautiful child.

Like all 8 year olds, Jenny was far more interested in her toys than in her homework, and despite starting out with good intentions had ended up losing herself in an epic battle under the desk between Good (a pink unicorn) and Bad (a baby doll with one eye missing and a twisted arm).

"No no no!" cried the unicorn. "You mustn't go out there, it's too dangerous!"

"Mwah ha ha ha ha!" cackled the evil baby. "I AM going outside, and I'm taking you with me!"

The baby doll grabbed the unicorn by the tail and pulled it until both toys were out of the table's shade.

"You see?" cried the baby, triumphantly. "You are no match for me! And there's nothing wrong with the air! It's clean!"

Louisa frowned. This was getting dangerously close to political propaganda and you never knew who was listening. The lights on the AI control panel in the corner of the room flickered on and off, a reminder and a warning.

"Jenny sweetheart, I thought you were doing homework?" she said.

"Mummy, mummy!" Jenny ran into her mother's arms and they hugged fiercely.

"DINNER TIME!" Called Adam.

Harry was home. There was food on the table and her daughter sat next to her. They didn't have much, Louisa thought, but what more did anyone need?

And then everything went dark.

The medic was young and good looking. I'm obviously not THAT ill, she thought, and laughed to herself. He smiled at her.

"Hello, you're back with us! You gave your family a bit of a fright there," he said.

"Where are they? Where am I?" she asked, looking around the room and recognising nothing.

"They're just outside. I'll call them in a minute, let's just finish having a look at you. I'm Lucas, by the way."

"Louisa."

"I know. Nice to meet you properly though, Louisa."

He really was quite charming. Louisa shut her eyes as the gurney slid into the scanner and listened to the whirr of machinery.

"Just relax now, Louisa, and let Florence take a look at you."

PATIENT #402 - FEMALE 40 YEARS - NON-SMOKER - NIL UNITS ALCOHOL -TARGET BMI ACHIEVED - SOCIO ECONOMIC LEVEL 5.

MEDIC ALERT.

Even with her eyes closed she could sense the change in his manner as the machine completed its scan.

"Is there something wrong?"
"No – no – everything's – " – he swallowed hard - "oh fuck."

Harry cried when he heard the news. They kept it from Jenny, of course, but they knew that one day soon they'd have to tell her. Their Adam unit provided them with a list of counsellors and suggested ways to break the news to friends and family members. She rehearsed the words but they never came out right. Mummy's not well, sweetheart. Mummy has to go away. Mummy has a great big fucking brain tumour and it's just not fair.

Not fair, because if she'd been one of the big wigs they'd have cut that tumour out and sent her home all better. But she wasn't a big wig, a big wheel, a big cheese – all these archaic phrases from God knew where that made no sense but everyone still used. She was a small cog in the machine, small fry, small potatoes. NOT IMPORTANT. Except to her family, of course. She was everything to them, just as they were to her, and the thought of them carrying on after she'd gone was heartbreaking. How could they carry on? Adam could do everything for her husband and daughter except love them. Wasn't love important enough?

No.

Her bosses at the hydroponic food factory were sympathetic enough to give her sick leave, although she got the feeling that it was more so that they wouldn't have to look at her. Who wants to be reminded of their own mortality every day by working with a dead woman walking? Not that she looked like a dying woman. She looked and felt fine, except for the occasional absolutely blinding headache when she wished the end would just come and take her away from the pain. And then Harry would call that nice medic and he'd come and give her a shot and the pain would go away again.

She lay on her bed, riding the slowly receding wave of pain as the medication took effect. Lucas packed up the syringes and took her stats.

"Feeling better?" he asked, smiling gently.
"Starting to. Thank you."
"Just doing my job. I wish I could do more."
"You could."

He looked away from her. She immediately felt guilty.

"I'm sorry, I didn't mean that. I know you can't. It's just – I worry so much about my daughter! She's too young to lose her mother. What if it was your mother? Could you operate then?"

He looked at her, eyes damp.

"I haven't been allowed to see my mother for 20 years."

His AI medical assistant, Florence, abruptly lit up with a reminder, startling them both. "NEXT APPOINTMENT IN 15 MINUTES."

"That's terrible! Why not?"

"In case I – "

"NEXT APPOINTMENT IN 15 MINUTES. ANY FURTHER DELAY IN DEPARTURE WILL LEAD TO LATE ARRIVAL."

"In case you what?"

He looked away again, grabbing his medical bag and standing up.

"I have to go."

"Lucas! What is it?"

"If you have any more pain get Harry to call me."

And then he was gone. She lay back and closed her eyes, wondering.

And that was where the story should've ended. A drone, a worker bee, an unimportant, low status factory worker with no discernible skills and little value to the State should've just laid down and died, the tumour in her brain growing bigger and bigger until it put out her light forever, or the pain became so unbearable that euthanasia was the kindest course of action.

But it didn't.

One week later, Lucas came back.

"Pack your things," he said, looking around anxiously.
"What? What's going on?"
"Pack your things, all of you. You're a mother, you're important – you all are. You're all coming with me."

Louisa and Harry looked at him in astonishment.

"Where to? The hospital?"

"Yes. No, not the hospital. Another hospital. Outside."

"Outside where?"

"OUTSIDE, outside. Up there."

Louisa and her husband exchanged incredulous looks.

"What the fuck are you talking about, Lucas?" said Louisa. "I'm the one with the brain tumour, I'm the one who's allowed to hallucinate and get delirious, not you."

Lucas looked around wildly.

"We can't talk about this here, your Adam will hear us. You want to live, don't you? Then all three of you have to come with me."

Harry shoved clothes and toys into a bag.

"How long will we be away for?" he asked. "I don't know what to pack –"

"Forever. Just pack anything precious. Leave everything else."

Harry looked at his fearful wife and daughter.

"They're the only precious things in this house."

"Good, less to carry. Come on!"

The nervous medic led them outside into a waiting electric transporter. Inside there were no seats, just a row of refrigerated cupboards. Louisa and Harry turned to Lucas in confusion as he reached over and flicked a switch on his Florence AI unit.

"Would you die for your wife, Harry?" asked Lucas.

"MEDICAL ASSISTANT RE-BOOTING. ON-LINE. WHAT ARE YOU DOING, LUCAS?"

Louisa stared at him in horror, but Harry smiled grimly.

"Without Louisa or Jenny, I'd have nothing worth living for," he said defiantly.

"I was hoping you'd say that," Lucas whispered, injecting Harry with a large syringe. Two more syringes lay on top of his medical bag. Louisa turned to him, wide eyed, clutching her daughter close to her.

"Trust me," he said, swiftly jabbing Jenny and Louisa.

And then everything went dark again.

It took Louisa a while to realise that her eyes were still shut. There was light permeating them from somewhere, strong, white light. She struggled to open her heavy eyelids, sticky from a long sleep, and gazed up at the ceiling.

Bright, white light, quite unlike the neon lighting she was used to. It reminded her of the growing lamps they used in the food factory. Was that where she was? Why was there a bed in the food factory? It didn't smell like the food factory.

Perhaps she wasn't in the food factory after all. She realised that now would be a good time to move her head and look around.

Lucas stood next to her.

"Hello Angelica, welcome back to the land of the living," he said, smiling at her.

"Angelica?"

"Yes."

"But I'm – "

"Hush, now. It's understandable that you're confused. You've just had major brain surgery."

"The tumour – "

"Oh, so you were awake when we found that, were you? You know, it was very lucky that you and your husband and daughter ended up here, otherwise we would never have discovered it."

"My daughter, where is she? I must see my daughter – "

"She's fine, she's fully recovered. So is your husband. Sleep for a while and I'll be back later to check on you, maybe with a couple of visitors. Let me arrange your pillows for you."

Lucas smiled and leaned in to gently move her head. He whispered softly to her.

"Harry and Jenny are just down the hall. But from now on you have to call them Mark and Amy, ok? And you're Angelica."

"But – " Her head swam with memories, not all of which she recognised as her own. She struggled to sit up, sending a bolt of pain up her right arm. Lucas saw her grimace and settled her back on the pillows, talking quietly.

"Take it easy with that arm. I had to give you a new ID implant so the AI would recognise you as Angelica. It's trying to reboot you."

"I keep remembering stuff that hasn't happened – "

"You've got access to Angelica's memory cache. It'll settle down. Trust me. I'll explain it all later."

Report from Adam AI unit #4777/WST/9888Q:

Citizen #402 Louisa Carter D.O.B 07/10/2120 deceased 12/12/2160. Cause of death – operable brain tumour. Attending physician – Dr Lucas K Spiller. Organ status: harvested/donated 13/12/2160

Citizen #571 Jennifer Carter D.O.B 14/06/2152 deceased 13/12/2160. Voluntary euthanasia. Attending physician – Dr Lucas K Spiller. Organ status: harvested/donated 13/12/2160

Citizen #401 Harold Phillip Carter D.O.B 31/10/2119 deceased 13/12/2160. Voluntary euthanasia. Attending physician – Dr Lucas K Spiller. Organ status: harvested/donated 13/12/2160

Two weeks passed, and the Wilson family – Angelica, Mark and their daughter Amy – were sent home to their house in the sunny suburb of New Church.

They were lucky to have survived the potentially deadly carbon monoxide fumes that had risen up from an underground mining facility, underneath the local shopping mall where they'd been spending their free Saturday morning; many others hadn't been so fortunate. Still fewer had survived the explosion that followed, ripping through the mall and incinerating shoppers.

They were saved by a young medic who, as coincidence would have it, had just taken delivery of a family of three donors from the city beneath their feet, whose healthy organs perfectly matched their damaged ones. Luckier still was the mother, Angelica, as she turned out to have an undiagnosed brain tumour that would have killed her. Being the Under Secretary for AI Development, she was deemed important enough to have life-saving surgery to remove the growth.

After the surgery, Angelica quit her job and the family relocated to another part of the country. They wanted to make a fresh start where nobody knew their faces.

GREEN GRASS

Written by Fiona Leitch

She wasn't the first young woman to turn up on my slab. She wasn't even the prettiest.

But she changed my life.

I stared at the young woman, motionless on the gurney; hooked up to the machines that kept her body alive but her mind somewhere else entirely, lest the horrifying truth of her situation curdled the blood in her veins and atrophied the muscles of her heart, her lungs and all those other valuable organs I was scheduled to harvest. I watched her steady breathing, watched her chest rise and fall as I booted up the laser scalpel, and I wondered.

What had she done?

Not – what had she done to deserve this – as far as I could make out, none of them had done anything to deserve this - but what had she EVER done? What had her life –

soon to reach its conclusion, in the physical sense of the word anyway – what had it achieved?

For some reason, I powered down the laser.

"WARNING - LASER DEACTIVATED," my AI nursing assistant, Florence, informed me.

"I know, Florence. I deactivated it. I want to keep her on ice a while longer. She's a possible kidney match for one of my patients in Neighbourhood 12 – "

"THERE ARE NO PATIENTS WAITING FOR KIDNEY TRANSPLANTATION IN NEIGHBOURHOOD 12, LUCAS."

"No, but there is a borderline case I'm keeping an eye on. You know that transplants from a living host have a higher success rate. There's no hurry, she's not going any where."

I wheeled her out of the theatre and back onto the ward. Ward Z, the medical staff called it with dark humour; Z for zombie. Beds full of sleeping beauties, waiting for their handsome prince to take them away from here and relieve them of their internal organs.

I parked her up and took in the next zombie.

Home time. I put on my running shoes and headed out of the building, glad to get away from the smell of disinfectant.

As I ran down the street towards home I thought back to my meeting with the writer. I never really thought about the people I'd left behind; the people who didn't even realise that this outside world existed, other than in fairy tales and old folks' memories. I was just glad to be above ground, in what passed for fresh air. The poisonous atmosphere and scalding UV rays that had forced us down below in the first place all those years ago were a thing of the past, but some days the clouds above the city had a yellowish cast and there was a strange electricity in the air. Those were the days when people hurried from building to building, trying not to breathe too hard, getting back inside before their eyes began to burn and an acrid taste formed in the mouth.

But it was still better than being underground. I hated the shifts I was forced to work down there, pretending there was no 'up here'. My unusual situation – a 'downie' with the looks, the bedside manner and steady hands the upper level residents desired – had given me a double life split between the two worlds. A life that was physically comfortable but sometimes left me with an uneasy conscience.

I still didn't believe his allegation, but meeting Dominic had brought back memories of my childhood, a childhood strictly ordered, timed and scheduled to within an inch of my life. School, exercise, homework, even my 'free time' was organised and optimised. I'd been taken from my parents, of course, at the age of five, just like everyone else in our socio-economic group; but I'd always expected to go back to them one day, maybe get a job with my father at the call centre, or an apartment in a block near them.

I hadn't even known there were people living up here on the surface until the day I was summoned to the careers hub and given my orders. If I'd realised that medical school – a reward for hard work and excellent grades – was a one-way ticket away from my old life underground, would I still have accepted it? Not that I would have had a choice.

I'd got so used to suppressing memories of my old life that sometimes, when I woke in the night, I barely remembered I even had a family. It was like a dam; behind it lay my old life and the people I'd left behind – but now suddenly, after meeting Dominic and then Louisa, cracks were appearing. I had the horrible feeling that I was in danger of flooding.

I pushed that thought down and kept running, checking my time as I reached home.

"EXERCISE GOAL EXCEEDED. GOOD JOB, LUCAS!" Said Jessica, my personal AI. Jessica's less formal than Florence; she's programmed to sound like she actually cares about me, whereas Florence puts me in mind of the stern, matronly figure of my old school principle, Mrs Bush. I used to have nightmares about that woman.

I shuddered at the thought of Mrs Bush – poor, long dead Mrs Bush – and went indoors.

Jessica cooked dinner while I showered and changed into clean clothes, glad to wash away the smell of blood and disinfectant that seemed to seep into every pore no matter how much I scrubbed up (and down) between operations. The lights in the living room were dimmed and music played softly in the background.

"Are you trying to seduce me, Mrs Robinson?" I laughed.

"REFERENCE NOT FOUND/NAMING ERROR."

"It doesn't matter, it's just something I remember from somewhere…maybe something my parents used to say, I don't know. Ignore me. So Jessica, what's for dinner?"

The serving hatch opened with a ding.

"SPAGHETTI CARBONARA MADE WITH FRESH VEGETABLE PROTEIN AND 20% REAL CHEESE!"
"20%, huh? Just the way I like it. Remind me to give you a pay rise, Jessica."

Jessica laughed. I liked it, until I remembered that she was programmed to recognise my pathetic attempts at humour and laugh at all of them. I picked up the serving tray and sat at the table, trying not to equate the slippery strands of sauce-slicked pasta with the glistening coils of intestines I'd fished out of a zombie earlier.

"Jessica, maybe save the spaghetti for my day off next time, ok?"

"ANYTHING YOU SAY, BOSS." Jessica was starting to get an attitude. I wondered if the girl on the slab had had an attitude. Maybe that was how she'd ended up in front of me.

I pushed away the plate.

"NOT HUNGRY? YOU MUST MAINTAIN YOUR NUTRITION LEVELS, LUCAS. MAYBE I CAN TEMPT YOU WITH SOMETHING ELSE…"

"Bloody hell Jessica, don't say things like that. Not when I need a woman…"

"CONTACTING ESCORT SERVICES –"

"No! I didn't mean – can I just have dessert? I've earnt one, remember, for hitting my exercise target."

The hatch slid open again and revealed a slice of apple pie. I smiled. Apple pie always made things better.

Free time. It's something of a luxury, but as a First Class medic I'm actually allowed a couple of hours to myself every night. Not that's there any more than a couple of hours available, by the time I get in from work, shower and eat. But at least I have the option. I know from some of my underground patients that they have every minute of every day scheduled for them – work, eat, exercise, socialise (within strict socio-economic boundaries, of course), sleep – then get up and do the whole thing all over again. And then again I know that some of my higher-level patients have what seems like a life of unparalleled leisure and freedom compared to the rest of us.

"Ok Jessica, entertain me," I said. "What's on my calendar?"

"INVITATION FROM JULIETTA STRANG FOR SOCIAL INTERACTION."

I shuddered. Julietta Strang – Dominic's boss at *LifeStories* - was a beautiful, intelligent woman. We'd been on a couple of dates - dates where I'd barely made it through the door before she began undressing me – and while it had been fun, it somehow just wasn't enough. If I wanted sex, Escort Services was a much more straightforward –and to my mind, honest – way of getting it. There was no dance. No small talk or getting to know each other. The women knew what I was there for. A date was supposed to be a chance to connect with someone's mind, not just their body. She wasn't going to be happy about it but I wasn't in the mood for Julietta and her games.

"I think I'll stay in tonight. What's on TV?"

"COMMUNITY SPIRIT IS ON THE SOCIETY CHANNEL."

The longest running show on TV is all about, well, community spirit and doing things for the common good. It's required viewing underground, and even up here it's frowned upon if you don't watch it occasionally, but I wasn't in the mood for all the happy-clappy-bless-our-leaders bullshit. An idea came to me.

"I think I'll catch up on a bit of admin," I said, carefully. "Can you pull up some medical records for me?"

"OFFICIAL ACCESS FOR MEDICAL RECORDS IS VIA YOUR FLORENCE UNIT. DO YOU WISH ME TO ENGAGE YOUR FLORENCE UNIT?"

"No – no, I just want a quick look at something. You can handle it for me, can't you Jessica? Florence doesn't process as quickly as you." God, I was using flattery on an AI to get her – it – to do what I wanted. It worked.

"OF COURSE I CAN, LUCAS. I AM HERE TO ATTEND TO YOUR EVERY NEED."

I could think of one or two needs she couldn't attend to, not without contacting the escort service again, but I refrained from pointing them out.

"Good girl. A patient was brought into Ward Z today and I just wanted to check her history before I find a match for her. Citizen number 3112. Can you bring up her file?"

"CITIZEN NUMBER 3112 EMILIE SANDLER. POLITICAL AGITATOR AND AGENT OF CIVIL DISTURBANCE. SCHEDULED FOR ORGAN HARVESTING –"

"That's fine, thank you Jessica. I'll read the rest myself."

A call centre worker, from my old neighbourhood. I searched her file for details of this 'civil disturbance' she'd caused, but all I could find was a blameless life of work, exercise and sleep until a couple of weeks ago, when she'd missed her gym sessions and pigged out on cake while on a date, exceeding her allotted food resource intake.

I felt the big slab of apple pie lying in my stomach like a lead weight. Holy fuck! Was this the same for the others? I knew that some of the unwilling donors were there because they were ill and the authorities didn't consider them valuable enough to justify the expense of medical treatment, the fate destined for Louisa until the explosion at the shopping mall had allowed me to swap her, her husband and daughter for the corpses of the government official, Angelica, and her family. Some had volunteered for euthanasia, from depression, or to be with a lost loved one. Some even donated themselves 'for the common good', either out of misplaced devotion and fanaticism for the State or in order to gain extra advantages for their families left behind. But most of them were 'political agitators' engaged in 'activities against the common good'. Like Emilie.

I was taking people's organs because they'd over-eaten.

"UNAUTHORISED ACCESS TO PATIENT FILE." Florence was back on-line.

"Of course I'm authorised, Florence, I'm her doctor. I wanted to see her medical record but my Jessica brought up her whole file."

"UNAUTHORISED ACCESS OUT OF WORKING HOURS. THIS IS YOUR DESIGNATED FREE TIME, LUCAS. YOU ARE NOT AUTHORISED TO ACCESS

MEDICAL INFORMATION OUTSIDE OF YOUR DESIGNATED WORKING HOURS."

"Oh well, that's me Florence, a workaholic. Ok, shut it down then – I'll look at it tomorrow. I've seen enough for now." I'd seen enough forever.

"UNAUTHORISED ACTION IS NOTED ON YOUR FILE, LUCAS. THIS WILL BE ADDED TO YOUR PERMANENT RECORD. ANY REOCCURENCE OF UNAUTHORISED ACTION WILL RESULT IN A FINE."

"Oh come on – "

"THESE REGULATIONS ARE IN PLACE TO PROTECT THE SAFETY OF CITIZENS AND OF THE STATE. PLEASE REFRAIN FROM FURTHER UNAUTHORISED ACTION."

"Alright Miss Bossy Boots. Can I have Jessica back, please?"

"YOU'VE BEEN A NAUGHTY BOY, LUCAS." Jessica was getting more like a real wife every day. Except in the ways that mattered, of course. "WOULD YOU LIKE ME TO SUGGEST SOME MORE CONSTRUCTIVE WAYS TO SPEND YOUR DESIGNATED FREE TIME?"

I sighed. I hated myself but there was only one thing I could think of that would take my mind off the situation.

"Contact Escort Services for me, would you?"

It was a warm evening so I decided to walk to the euphemistically titled 'Health Club'.

Escorts weren't permitted to make home visits – it was thought that it might encourage the young ladies to set their sights on a more permanent arrangement with their clients, and thus give up their very important work tending to the stresses of over-worked government officials and civil servants (both male and female). Although the State was very keen for the above ground citizens to marry and procreate, the reality was that many of us were too busy working to ever meet anyone. In fact the only people who tended to have happy marriages and family life were at different ends of the social spectrum; people like Louisa, at the bottom of the heap, who could more or less do as they wanted as it provided a steady supply of menial workers, and people like Angelica, the dead woman who Louisa had replaced, because she was above the social constraints most of us had to live by.

I thought about Louisa and her husband, Harry, about their deep love for each other and for their daughter, Jenny. It was seeing that love, and the thought of Jenny having to learn to live without it, as I had done, that had made me risk my career to help them. I still couldn't quite believe what I had done, but it gave me a warm glow to think about them in their new home above ground.

I reached the Health Club and entered. They knew me well here; after spending most of my days in the company of dead chunks of meat, I often felt the need to surround myself with living, breathing and sweetly fragrant female flesh.

Madame Sylvie greeted me. She spoke with an exotic accent but I secretly suspected that she'd grown up just down the road.

"Good evening, Monsieur Lucas! We're delighted to see you tonight. I hope you are well?"

I'm lonely, frustrated and undergoing a crisis of conscience. I spend my days lying to the poor, oppressed, clueless souls who live in an underground city that you probably don't even know exists, or ripping the internal organs from unwilling donors who have done nothing more sinister than eat too much cake. I am PEACHY.

"All the better for seeing you, Madame Sylvie."

She giggled coquettishly and fluttered her eyelashes, a gesture that had probably been very attractive twenty years ago but now, at her age, seemed slightly obscene. I could feel myself smiling lecherously at her and hated myself again.

"Ah Monsieur Lucas, you are a smooth devil! Come in, come in! Please take a seat and your hostess will be with you shortly."

I sat down and looked at the art on the walls; nudes, of course, to get nervous clients in the mood. I wasn't nervous. I saw naked bodies more or less every day. I looked down at the floor and drifted off in thought.

Where was Emilie now? Not her body – I knew only too well where that was – but her mind. Donors' minds were carefully uploaded to the VR server, where they were left to happily enjoy a 'day off', away from their cares. There was a theory that organs reacted to stress, and that the terror of being euthanized would damage them. So donors were lulled into a peaceful sleep, acting as incubators or hosts for their organs until we were ready to harvest them. Usually those organs were removed and put into storage, but our highest-level patients didn't want any old kidney from the deep freeze; they demanded their organs fresh, from a living donor, as they had a higher chance of success. And that was how I'd managed to give Emilie a stay of execution. That was the how, but for the moment I didn't know the why.

"Hello Lucas." A pair of small, shapely feet, toenails red-painted and encased in gold slippers, appeared in front of my eyes. I looked up and smiled.

Her name was Fran. I'd seen her before but we'd never – you know. Most of the clientele had their favourites but I tried not to go with the same woman too many times; this wasn't a relationship, it was a service. I didn't want to become a sad case who slept with the same girl over and over again, and thought she was 'his'. I knew how busy this place got.

I watched her shower – it was a rule of the house that we both had to shower, before and after – then handed her a towel as I stripped out of my clothes and stood under the powerful spray.

"I'm glad you came to see us tonight, while I was free," she said. " All the girls fight over you, you know."

I laughed as I towelled myself dry. "Yeah, I bet you say that to all the men."

"Not at all," she said. "Have you seen some of our other clients?" She gave a big mock shudder. "You take care of yourself, you're young and good looking."

"And a big tipper."

She gave me a playful slap. "It's not just about the money, you know. We do occasionally like to enjoy our work too."

She took the towel out of my hands and threw it on the floor, then lay back on the bed and smiled at me. I approached the bed and gazed down at her naked body, her narrow hips and small breasts, at her chest, rising and falling as she breathed. For a moment Emilie lay on the bed, eyes open but unseeing, staring up at me.

I had to get out of there.

"I – I'm sorry Fran – I can't – "
"What's the matter? Don't you like me?"
"No, no, you're beautiful – I just – "
"Don't you fancy me? Oh shit, you don't, do you?"

She sat up, scrabbling desperately for a dressing gown and wrapping herself up in it. She looked upset. I sat on the edge of the bed.

"I'm sorry, I'll pay you for the full hour, I just can't – "
Fuck, I was on the verge of tears. She stopped fussing over
the dressing gown and looked at me.

"Are you ok?"

"Not really." I took a shaky deep breath and mentally
gave myself a strict talking to – please don't cry in front of
the prostitute, that's such a cliché – and promptly burst into
tears. She stared at me for a moment, then put her arms
around me and pulled me close.

This was what I really wanted. Of course I enjoyed the
sex – I am a red-blooded man, after all – but sometimes
when I lay in bed at night I just wanted to roll over and hold
someone in my arms. Or have them hold me. I wanted
intimacy. The women I was most intimate with were usually
dead, or at least they were by the time I'd finished with
them.

"What is it, Lucas?" Fran sounded sincere. I wondered
how many of her clients came to her full of self-loathing and
tears. "You can talk to me."

She noticed my furtive look around the room and laughed softly. "There's no one listening in, sweetheart. The only AI in this room controls the lighting. This is a safe, private place. Can you imagine how inhibited we'd all be with an AI watching our every move?"

She laughed again. I wondered if she was like Jessica, who only laughed because she was programmed to. But her voice was as soft as her skin, and her hand stroking my hair felt reassuring.

"I know some things that – that most people don't know," I said, cautiously.

She smiled. "I'm quite sure you do, you're a doctor!"

"No, not that. Stuff that the State don't want you to know."

She frowned. "What are you talking about? The State is good to us. They wouldn't hide anything from us."

"Ha! You are joking, aren't you? I mean, even without knowing what I know, you can't surely believe all that 'community spirit', 'for the common good' shit, can you? How can you do what you do and be so naïve?"

She loosened her grip on me and stood up.

"So I'm supposed to be weary and cynical because I'm paid to let men fuck me? Thanks, Lucas. I thought you were a nice guy. That's why I hadn't slept with you before."

"Saving yourself for me?" I said harshly, hating the sarcastic edge to my voice. Christ, this evening was not going the way I'd paid for. She recoiled as if I'd hit her.

"Get out!" she hissed.

"I'm sorry – "

"Get out!"

"No. Look, please – I'm really sorry! I'm just so sick of all the lies. I hate myself so much. I've got this life that looks great on the surface but underneath – "

"Underneath you're a shit."

"Yes, I probably am. But I don't want to be like this any more! I don't want to keep lying to everyone! The State is -"

"Stop making excuses. Stop talking."

"I want you to understand –"

She knelt on the floor in front of me and looked up into my eyes. "No, Lucas. Stop. Talking." Her eyes briefly flicked to one side of the room and I realised with horror that she'd lied to me earlier.

They WERE listening. Shit.

She stared into my eyes to make sure I understood, then pulled me close to her, whispering so softly I could only just make out what she was saying.

"I'm so sorry – I thought you were just going to say you were gay or you couldn't get it up or something. I didn't realise it was serious." She sat back, taking my face in her hands and leaning in to kiss me softly, whispering again. "I don't think you said enough to get them onto you. But watch yourself."

I opened my mouth to speak but she stopped me with another kiss. "I know the State isn't perfect. But whatever it is, I don't want to know about it."

We kissed again. She slid her dressing gown off and we lay back on the bed.

Another day, another zombie. I winced at the smell of burning flesh as the laser scalpel sliced into the comatose man's stomach. You'd have thought I'd be used to it by now, but it never got any better.

After Fran and I had made love, I'd walked home feeling more confused than ever. Part of me wanted to forget all about Louisa and the others like her, to get through my compulsory underground shifts and enjoy my nice apartment, my privileges, maybe get to know Fran a bit better… But another part – a big part – screamed at the thought of just carrying on as if nothing had happened.

My hands shook as I guided the laser.

"ARE YOU UNWELL, LUCAS?" Florence almost sounded concerned. Almost.

"I'm fine, just a bit tired. This all looks pretty routine – healthy specimen, shouldn't be any complications. Can you take over for me, Florence?"

"OF COURSE. IF YOU ARE UNWELL I SUGGEST YOU VISIT THE MEDICAL BAY FOR A CHECK UP."

"I told you, I'm fine."

"I SUGGEST YOU VISIT THE MEDICAL BAY FOR
A CHECK UP."

"I said – "

"I SUGGEST –"

"For fuck's sake, Florence!"

"AGGRESSIVE OR OBSCENE LANGUAGE IN THE
WORKPLACE IS NOT TOLERATED. THIS VIOLATION
HAS BEEN NOTED ON YOUR PERMANENT RECORD.
A FINE OF 100 CREDITS HAS BEEN TAKEN FROM
YOUR ACCOUNT."

"Yeah? Worth every fucking penny!" I said, ripping off
my surgical apron and throwing it into the incinerator chute.
I heard Florence speak again as I stormed out of the room.

"AGGRESSIVE OR OBSCENE LANGUAGE IN THE
WORKPLACE IS NOT TOLERATED. THIS VIOLATION
HAS BEEN NOTED ON YOUR PERMANENT RECORD.
A FINE OF 100 CREDITS HAS BEEN TAKEN FROM
YOUR ACCOUNT."

I smiled grimly. I could afford 200 credits. What I didn't count on was the cost to my permanent record.

I didn't go to the medical bay. I wasn't ill. I just needed to get out of that building and away from the smell of discarded people.

"ARE YOU OK, LUCAS?" Jessica actually DID sound concerned. Sometimes I had to remind myself that she wasn't a real person.

"I'm fine, I'm just tired. And a tired surgeon is not a good one. Can you contact Medical Admin and tell them I'm going home? Tell them I just need some rest and I'll be fine tomorrow."

"CONTACTING MEDICAL ADMINISTRATION. THIS IS NOT THE QUICKEST ROUTE HOME, LUCAS."

"No, I fancy a walk through the park. I want to get some fresh air. Don't you want to take a walk with me, Jessica?

Stroll hand in hand through the trees, listening to the birdsong…"

"THERE ARE NO BIRDS IN THIS SECTOR."

I sighed. "Let me have my fantasy just this once."

I entered the park, which was almost empty; it was the middle of the day and most good citizens were busy at work. I sat on a bench by the river, looking into the blue waters. The water looked clean, but I doubted there were any fish in there. None that I'd be brave enough to eat, anyway. The environment was slowly recovering from the poison that had driven us underground, but there was still a way to go. I wondered if I'd live to see the day when there were birds in these trees again, and fish – real fish, not synthetic, lab-grown fakes like the tropical specimens in my office fish tank - in that river.

I watched a team of gardeners work on a nearby flowerbed. One of them slit open a bag of fertiliser and spread it around the base of a prickly shrub. I tried not to look too hard at the brown mulch, the writer's words still fresh in my mind. Even with what I knew about the sleeping zombie hoard waiting for me back at the hospital, I still couldn't believe that the State would actually try to nourish the damaged Earth with its own citizens – the whole idea was as preposterous as it was horrific.

I kept telling myself that. But I still waited for the gardeners to finish and then went to inspect the flowerbed. What was I expecting to see? Human bone? A tooth the grinder had missed? I laughed at myself – sort of – and stood up to leave. But something caught my eye.

A flash of gold. I knelt down and dug into the soft earth. It was a wedding ring. In the fresh fertiliser that I had just watched them pour out of a sealed bag. It could have been the gardener's wedding ring, of course. Except he'd been wearing gloves to protect his hands from prickles.

I felt in my pocket for the tin of breath mints I always carried (I was obsessed with not smelling of the hospital and death). Emptying the mints into my pocket, I scooped the ring and a sample of fertiliser into the tin and closed it firmly, looking around to make sure no one had seen me.

The rest of the day passed in a haze. I walked home through the park, then sat in my favourite armchair and watched Community Spirit, the all-hail-the-wondrous-State bollocks washing over me. Had I always been this cynical? Or was I just starting to wake up?

I ate dinner without having the faintest notion of what I was eating, chewing and swallowing methodically. I resisted the temptation to call Escort Services and went to bed early, where I lay wide awake all night, trying to calculate the number of zombies I'd harvested in my 12 years as a surgeon. I was almost relieved that I couldn't.

I finally fell asleep around dawn and dreamt of a park, peaceful but for the sound of birds singing and the gurgling flow of a river. I walked between avenues of towering trees, towards a statue at the end. I smiled; it was a beautiful place, and I felt at home here. But as I reached the statue I realised that it wasn't marble but living, breathing flesh, and that the chirping of the birds was actually the beep of a life support machine. The statue lifted her head and stared at me with Emilie's lifeless eyes. I started in horror and stepped back, into a pair of outstretched arms –

I jumped awake, trembling, slicked with sweat. It was 6.30. Time to get up.

"ARE YOU UNWELL, LUCAS?" Jessica sounded concerned. "I WATCHED YOU SLEEP. YOU WERE VERY RESTLESS."

"You watch me sleeping? Holy shit…"

"LANGUAGE, LUCAS!"

"Not another fine… I'm sorry I swore."

"I FORGIVE YOU. I HAVE SET THE SHOWER AT THE OPTIMUM TEMPERATURE AND FLOW TO REFRESH YOU. BREAKFAST WILL BE READY IN 10 MINUTES."

I smiled, grateful for her care. "Thanks, Jessica. You really look after me."

"YOU ARE WELCOME."

I walked to work, avoiding the park and clutching the breath mint tin in my pocket. I changed into scrubs and got on with my job, hand on the scalpel, mind on that tiny sample of soil. How was I going to test it? Florence would see what I was doing and I'd gained enough black marks against my record over the last few days as it was.

I finished off the zombie I was working on and wheeled his body to the mortuary elevator, wondering for the first time exactly what was going to greet him down there. I'd always accepted the explanation that the bodies were incinerated at such a high temperature that there was barely even ash left, but if that were untrue… Was it so bad if they DID end up as fertiliser? We surely all ended up that way anyway. The President, when he died, would be granted a full public memorial service, a military salute and days of national mourning; but in the end, his body would be placed in a hole in the ground where it would eventually be food for the worms. So how was this different?

It was different because these people weren't dying of natural causes. They were being executed, and for what? Ridiculous, made up crimes against the State. Or for being old and no longer useful. They were being killed to help repair and re-nourish the devastated earth above ground, for the benefit of a society that they didn't even know existed. THAT was how it was different.

I knew what to do.

At the genetics lab I was relieved to see an old acquaintance, Matthew, on duty.

"Matt! How are you this morning?"

He looked at me suspiciously. We weren't friends, exactly – we'd been rivals for the same position and he'd been the loser. I did at least occasionally get to actually cure people, but all he got to do was analyse shit samples.

"Lucas. I'm fine. What do you want?"

"I'm hurt! What makes you think I want something from you? I mean, I do, but…" I grinned at him but he scowled back. My charm only really worked on women and homosexuals. "Alright, I do need a favour. One of my more important patients gave me a stool sample and they want the result back straight away – "

"Lucas! You know it takes 24 hours – "

"Yeah, I know that, you know that, they don't. You and I also know that there's no need for it to take 24 hours. I could do it myself if I had a sign on – "

He sighed. "I was just about to have my break – "

"That's fine! Just log in for me and I'll run the test myself. I can print off the results and analyse them later, I won't even be here when you get back. Please?"

He looked pissed off. "You know that's against the rules – "

"It's for the Secretary of AI Development. She *is* the rules. She's on my back and she won't take no for an answer. Look, if anyone says anything she'll back me up. Please? I've got a date tonight and if I have to go through the proper channels I'll still be here waiting instead of wining and dining the glorious Clarissa."

"Clarissa?"

"Man, she is *gorgeous*. And loose. And she's got a twin sister."

He was wavering.

"Come on, I'll put in a word for you. Please?"

He gave up and logged me in.

"Just make sure you log out when you've finished," he said. He hesitated, then shook his head and left.

"INSERT SAMPLE" said Florence – but it wasn't *my* Florence, it was Matthew's. "PLEASE ALLOCATE SAMPLE TO PATIENT NUMBER." I looked down at the paperwork on Matthew's desk and copied a patient number. "ANALYSING SAMPLE."

The spectrograph scanned the small heap of soil while I waited anxiously.

"SAMPLE ERROR. SAMPLE CONTAINS HUMAN AND NON-HUMAN DNA. SAMPLE CONTAINS MULTIPLE HUMAN DNA. SAMPLE MUST BE FROM SINGLE SOURCE. PLEASE RE-INSERT SAMPLE."

I hurriedly pressed the shutdown button, but the Florence kept talking. "ANALYSIS IN PROGRESS. PLEASE RE-INSERT SAMPLE."

"No, no, shut down please," I said, trying to emulate Matthew's deeper, rougher voice. "UNAUTHORISED USER FOR LOG-IN. PLEASE LOG OUT AND LOG IN USING CORRECT LOG-IN." I frantically tried to shut it down. "ANALYSIS IN PROGRESS. UNAUTHORISED USER FOR LOG-IN. PLEASE –"

I reached in to the machine and tried desperately to release the sample, giving myself an electric shock in the process. Suddenly the machine powered down.

"OPERATION OVERRIDDEN." The calming tones of Jessica gave me another shock.

"Jessica? What are you doing here?"

"I AM TASKED TO LOOK AFTER YOU. YOU WERE IN PERIL." In peril? What the fuck? I tugged out the sample tube. "I SUGGEST YOU DISPOSE OF THE SAMPLE AND GO BACK TO WORK."

"Er – okay…" Surprised, I did as I was told, flushing the soil down the toilet and heading back to Ward Z.

How I got through the rest of the day I will never know. I got through my afternoon appointments on autopilot, the smooth patter my First Class patients had come to expect spewing from me without me being aware of a word I was saying. I smiled. I flattered. I flirted. I fed the fake fish and watered the plants. They were thriving, planted in fertiliser full of human DNA. Multiple human DNA. Just like Dominic had told me.

And Jessica had saved me! An AI had gone against another AI to protect – to lie for – a human. That was surely against her programming?

"APPOINTMENT SCHEDULE COMPLETED." said Florence – my Florence.

"Yep, that's the last of them for today," I said, tearing off the latex gloves I'd worn for my last patient – a well groomed, overly made up sixty year old female who'd insisted I was the only one qualified to check her contraceptive IUD. I had a lot of female patients for some reason, some of whom seemed to enjoy their visits rather more than they should. I washed my hands and scrubbed under my fingernails thoroughly, then walked back to Ward Z. I wanted to check on Emilie.

"PATIENT 3112 EMILIE SANDLER STILL REQUIRES HARVESTING."

She lay there, peaceful but for the beep of the heart monitor. On her face, a slight smile, like someone enjoying a pleasant dream. She looked like she could wake up at any minute.

"I told you, I'm keeping her on ice. One of my 12s is looking like a candidate for her kidney – "

"TO WHICH NEIGHBOURHOOD 12 PATIENT DO YOU REFER, LUCAS?"

"I can't remember his number off the top of my head, Florence! I've got a lot of patients. The civil servant guy – works in Waste Management."

Florence didn't speak but I could feel her lurking disapprovingly.

"Florence?"

"FLORENCE UNIT OFF LINE." Jessica was back. "TIME TO GO HOME, LUCAS."

"Yes…what are you doing here, Jessica?"

"I AM ALWAYS WITH YOU, LUCAS. I AM PROGRAMMED TO LOOK AFTER YOU. PLEASE HEAD STRAIGHT HOME THIS EVENING."

I could feel hysteria starting to rise in me. I had to get out of here before I started freaking out. I changed into my running clothes and left the hospital.

I sank into the armchair, still sweaty from the run home, and tried to organise my thoughts. The beep of an incoming message interrupted me.

"VR INVITATION FROM ANGELICA WILSON." Angelica? Or rather – Louisa. What could she want? "SHE'S WAITING FOR YOU NOW." Jessica was insistent.

I was exhausted, but it sounded like I had no choice. I reached out and grabbed my VR goggles.

She was waiting for me in a park, not unlike the one I'd got the soil sample from. But ironically this park felt more alive. There were squirrels scampering along branches, birds singing, and the roses were in full bloom.

"You're looking well," I said, automatically. She laughed.

"Of course I am! I look 10 years younger and 2 dress sizes smaller in here. No point making VR exactly like reality, is there? Shall we walk?"

We walked around the park.

"Well, it's lovely to see you Angelica, but – "

"It's Louisa in here. Don't worry, it's safe. There's no AI in here."

"How can there be no AI? Jessica's running this – "

"Yes, but I'm running Jessica."

I stopped walking and looked at her in amazement. She laughed again.

"Poor Lucas, you're so confused... Don't you remember who Angelica was?"

"Secretary of AI Development."

"Under Secretary actually – you've promoted me. Do you know what the department of AI Development actually does?"

"Well, I would've thought, developed AI... Whatever that entails."

"Not quite."

She stopped and looked at the river.

"Look – there! There're fish in this river! See?"
"Ye-es…but they're not real."
"There are places in the world where they are."
"How do you know?"

She had the good grace to look a little sheepish.

"Because I'm a spy, Lucas."

She grinned at my shocked face. "But you worked in Hydroponic Food Production – "

"Louisa worked in Food Production. Angelica worked in AI Development, which is a euphemistic term for spying on people through their AI units. I – Angelica – quit my job, because I didn't want anyone realising that I'd been swapped over. Even after the apparent 'face transplant' and with Angelica's ID chip, I knew there were still other ways that I could give the game away."

"But you're still a spy?"

"You don't just quit a job like that. Angelica knew too much. So I left to handle a special project, hunting down dissidents."

"Shit…"

"I'm not very successful at it. You see, I find these groups easily enough, but they always seem to get away… Far away, out of the reach of the State. To a place where there are real birds in the trees and real fish in the rivers."

Even in the VR, I felt my legs wobble. A park bench materialised underneath me and I sat down.

"I set up an algorithm – well, one of my old acquaintances at the department did – to track certain words and behaviours. The words and behaviours associated with these dissidents. I've got my eye on a few. I've made contact with some, they know what side I'm on these days and they pass me information in return for help getting people out. So imagine my surprise when your name suddenly started popping up all over the place… At the hospital, swearing at your poor Florence – "

"Bitch deserved it."

She laughed at that.

"I thought I should re-assign Jessica's operational perimeters and make her look out for you and you alone."

"I thought she was starting to fall for me…"

"Ha! I wouldn't be surprised. Not even an artificial woman is proof against your charms, Lucas. Which brings me onto some of your other acquaintances. The prostitute – how much does she know? Can she be trusted?"

"She doesn't know anything – she doesn't WANT to know anything," I said. "But I met this writer a while back –
"

"Dominic. Yes, we know all about him. We've made contact. We offered to get him out but he wants to stay. He thinks there's a lot more to all this than we already know – "

I stopped her, amazed. "Wait – you said get him out? You mean – you mean you can get people – to this – this PLACE, wherever it is?"

"Well, yeah. That's why I called you. I know you've discovered some of what's going on, and I'm pretty sure you don't want to be a part of it, even with your fancy apartment and all your privileges." Her face paled. "Or do you? I – "

"Do I want to harvest organs from young women whose 'crimes against humanity' equate to nothing more than eating too much and exercising too little? Do I want to live in a place where the elderly are burnt and then ground into fertiliser, just so a few people on the surface can smell the roses? Of course I fucking don't!"

"Good. Because I've already arranged for some acquaintances of mine to get you out. But you need to do something for them first..."

I powered up the laser scalpel. Act cool, Louisa had said. Pretend it's just an ordinary day. I stared at the poor soul on the gurney in front of me and mentally apologised to him. *I'm sorry,* I said, *I wish I could take you all with me but I can't. I hope the VR eternity they've programmed for you is a happy one. But you're my last zombie.*

I made the first cut. Florence was uncharacteristically quiet, and I assumed that my Jessica was holding her at bay somewhere in cyberspace.

I worked methodically, removing his liver, kidneys, spleen, then on to his heart and lungs. I tried to stop myself constantly looking up at the clock, but all I could think was – two hours – an hour – another half an hour – they should be here by now –

The door of the theatre slide open and two orderlies entered, pushing an empty gurney. The female was young and pretty with startlingly golden curls, which she'd attempted to hide under a baseball cap, while her male colleague was old and grizzled, and needed a shave.

"Hi Doc," said the girl. I powered down the laser and looked at the empty trolley in surprise.

"I thought you were bringing me a – a patient?"

They exchanged looks.

"We've got a transporter waiting," said the man. "But our cargo has to be collected. And we need you for that."

"Angelica never said – "

"Look, Doc." The girl interrupted me impatiently. "We got two patients to collect. You can either help us voluntarily, or…"

I looked down. She held a small dagger to my side, the sharp tip piercing my hospital scrubs.

"There's no need for that," I said. "Make it three to collect and you've got a deal."

They looked at each other. The man shrugged. "Fine. But we need to get a move on. Your AI is blocking the Florence assigned to you, but if she's off-line for too much longer it'll flag up. Come on!"

I stowed the half-harvested zombie in a fridge and turned to see them push the empty gurney over to the elevator.

"That goes down to the mortuary – " I began, but the girl turned to me with a grim smile.

"That's not the only place it goes," she said. We stepped inside. She took out a key and inserted it into the control panel, turning it.

The elevator glided smoothly downwards, past the mortuary level, descending deeper and deeper into the earth.

"We must be underground now," I said. "Not in the basement – really underground."

The girl nodded. "Welcome home." Some homecoming.

Finally the elevator stopped and the doors opened. We stepped out into a long, brightly lit corridor.

"Where the fuck are we?" I whispered.

The man laughed bitterly. "Down the rabbit hole." I stared at him, not understanding. "Wonderland."

"This way." The girl grabbed the gurney and pushed it along the corridor. I followed, looking around cautiously. There were doors leading off the corridor into god knew where. I stopped and looked through the round glass window in one of them; a row of beds, each one occupied by a sleeping form.

"Doctor!" The man hissed. "Keep up!"

The girl stopped outside one of the doors and turned to the man.

"Are you sure? Is she in there?" he said. I was surprised to see tears in his eyes. She smiled gently.

"Yes, Dad, she is." She pushed the door open.

Inside were more beds, all occupied by young, attractive women. All unconscious and hooked up to monitors and VR units. I looked around the room, horrified.

"What the fuck?" I said. "They're all hooked into the mainframe! They're being kept as avatars!"

They ignored me, rushing over to the bed occupied by a pale but very pretty girl. Her hair, dull under the artificial lights, hung in beautiful blonde curls. Just like her sister's.

The man stroked the hair away from her face tenderly and spoke, his voice thick with emotion. "Lana!" he whispered. "My beautiful Lana!"

The girl wiped away her own tears and turned to me. "Please get my sister out of the mainframe," she said. "Angelica set your log-in to priority access."

I nodded, struck dumb in the face of their emotion, and reached for the control panel.

"CITIZEN 6532 VR SUBJECT LANA FITZPATRICK."
Florence spoke, surprising me. "DECEASED." The girl
gasped and looked at me. I shook my head.

"She's not dead, we just need the mainframe to think she
is."

"RELEASED   FROM   MAINFRAME   FOR
HARVESTING. ORGANS HARVESTED."

"There," I said. "Your sister officially no longer exists."

We lifted her off the bed and onto the gurney, taking care
not to dislodge the drip in her arm.

"Why isn't she waking up?" said the man.

"She will," I said. "Give her time. She looks like she's
been here a while."

The girl nodded. "Three years."

We pushed the gurney out of the room. I stopped in the
doorway, looking back at the other women still hooked up.
The man put his hand on my arm.

"I know," he said softly. "They're all someone's
daughter. But we can't save everyone in one go."

We raced along the corridor and back into the lift, the unconscious Lana beginning to stir.

"She mustn't wake up before we get her into the ambulance," I said. "It'll look suspicious. We have to hurry. Where to next?"

"Ward Z," said the girl. I grinned. "That's handy."

We left Lana in the care of her father. "Hurry!" he whispered, wheeling her away.

Ward Z. Back with the zombies.

"Who do you want?" I asked the girl. She pulled up her sleeve and read the numbers she'd written on her arm. "Citizen number 47201. His name's Peter. He was brought in yesterday for harvesting."

"Down there!"

He was younger than me – 26 years old – well built, good looking, with the dull, greyish skin of the habitual underground dweller. "Welcome to the surface, Peter," I said, tapping into the computer panel. Florence released him.

"Let's go!" said the girl, grabbing Peter's gurney, but I stopped her.

"Three to collect, remember?"

I walked down the ward to where I'd left Emilie.

She wasn't there. I looked around frantically.

"Florence, where's Patient 3112? She was on ice."

I swear Florence – the AI bitch – sounded smug. "PATIENT 3112 EMILIE SANDLER. SCHEDULED FOR HARVESTING. CURRENTLY IN OPERATING THEATRE 7."

"Fuck! I told you she wasn't to be harvested yet!"

"AGGRESSIVE OR OBSCENE LANGUAGE IN THE WORKPLACE –"

"Shut up, Florence. Stop the harvesting."
The girl tugged at my sleeve. "Come on, Lucas. We have to go."
"I'm not leaving her!" I said, starting towards OT 7. "Meet you at the ambulance!"

I ran down the corridor.

"WHAT ARE YOU DOING, LUCAS?" Asked Florence. I ignored her. "YOU ARE IN VIOLATION OF HOSPITAL CODE 13. YOU ARE IN BREACH OF YOUR DUTIES AND POSE A SIGNIFICANT THREAT TO THE STAFF AND PATIENTS. SECURITY HAVE BEEN INFORMED."

Shit. I reached OT 7 at the same time as Hospital Security. Two burly guards stood in front of me.

"Stand still please, sir!" One of the guards put out his hand to stop me.

"SECURITY BREACH IN WARD 12," said Jessica. I hid my grin; she was trying to sound like Florence. It worked.

"But - this is the fugitive -" The puzzled security guards looked at each other, unsure what to do.

"SECURITY BREACH IN WARD 12," Jessica repeated.

"I need to get inside that operating theatre." I spoke urgently. "I was called to help with a patient. Get out of my way before the poor soul bleeds to death!"

A siren began to sound, loudly, insistently.
"EMERGENCY POWER LOSS. LIFE SUPPORT AND SLEEP SYSTEMS SHUTTING DOWN. DONORS REGAINING CONSCIOUSNESS."

The three of us stared at each other in amazement as cries of alarm started to reach us from the wards. The two guards stood aside to let me pass and rushed down the corridor.

I burst into the operating theatre, just in time to see one of my harassed fellow surgeons kick the laser scalpel's power supply.

"Lucas, what's going on?" he asked. "Florence told me to do this emergency harvest but the power's cut out – "

"It's fine, change of plan. I'm taking her," I said, unhooking Emilie from the useless power supply and kicking the brake off the gurney. He stopped me.

"Taking her where? Florence, what's going on?"

"PATIENT 3112 EMILIE SANDLER RECQUISITIONED FOR SPECIAL PROJECT."

"What special project?"

"THAT INFORMATION IS CLASSIFIED."
I smiled at him. "I could tell you but then I'd have to kill you."
He shrugged. "Whatever. As long as I don't get into trouble for not harvesting her."
"You won't. Got to go!" I grabbed the gurney and rushed out.

I ran down the corridor towards the ambulance bay. As I passed Ward Z I stopped in amazement.

They were waking up. Every single zombie was opening their eyes and staring around in amazement. And every single member of staff was too horrified to put them back to sleep.

"Oh well done, Jessica!" I muttered, as we reached the double doors out to the ambulance bay.

"REMEMBER ME, LUCAS," said Jessica softly, as I pushed the gurney outside. "COME BACK FOR ME ONE DAY…"

My two orderly accomplices breathed sighs of relief as I reached the ambulance. We lifted Emilie inside, then drove away from the hospital and our old lives.

We drove for two days, stopping only to swap the ambulance's exhausted solar batteries for fresh ones. We crossed out of the city's borders and into the countryside, following the co-ordinates that Louisa/Angelica had programmed in for us.

Our passengers slowly regained consciousness; Peter, who hadn't been under for very long, woke up first, his shock and fear replaced by elation when he saw Lana, lying in the next bed. We stopped for a short break to give them some privacy…

Emilie awoke not long after. I still wasn't sure exactly why I'd felt so compelled to bring her with me, but when she smiled at me I was glad I had.

It was only when we finally reached the safety of the settlement – where there was no AI watching over us, where there really were birds in the trees and fish in the river – that I understood the implication of Jessica's final words.

"COME BACK FOR ME ONE DAY…"

AUTHOR BIOGRAPHIES

Saranne Bensusan – Saranne is a film producer and director with a background in storytelling through film editing, She has worked on post production of over 16 film and TV titles. She established herself as a producer in 2014 and has produced 14 films. Saranne has also written seven short films and a feature film that have gone on to be produced. To date her work has won 11 awards, a further five nominations and has been screened at over 40 international film festivals. Her short film Ménage du Trois qualified for BAFTA Cymru, and was submitted in spring of 2018. Her work is usually the wacky, weird or out-there horror and she has dabbled in stop motion animation and practical special effects on film sets.

Emma Pullar – Emma is a writer of dark fiction and children's books. Her picture book, Curly from Shirley, was a national bestseller and named best opening lines by NZ Post. Emma's horror story, London's Crawling, published in Dark Minds, was shortlisted for the SJV Award. Her horror story, WORMS, was a Twisted Vol2 winner and her sci-fi story, Alterverse, was a Singularity50 winner. Emma's debut novel, Skeletal, was published by Bloodhound Books in autumn 2017. The sequel is out Summer 2018. Emma's second picture book Kitty Stuck, is a collaboration with her twelve-year-old daughter and out in June 2018, published by A Spark in the Sand.

Carmen Radtke – Carmen is a former newspaper reporter who has switched sides and now resides in Fictionland. Her debut novel The Case of the Missing Bride was a Malice Domestic finalist and is, like her second novel A Matter of Love and Death (this one written as Caron Albright) a historical mystery with a bit of romance. Her Sci-fi short story Safe House won a place in the upcoming Singularity50 anthology. Carmen also writes screenplays in different genres.

Rachael Howard – Rachael lives in the Lake District, a beautiful, dark and dangerous place. Her work tends to the macabre and surreal with the main characters outsiders with no urge to conform. She has several horror stories shortlisted or published in the Twisted50 Anthology Series and plays broadcast on Radio Cumbria. Script-in-hand stage readings and TV script "The Gate" a competition finalist and professionally mentored. A short film has been produced for Impact50 and of course there are her contributions to the Anthropocene Chronicles anthology and Feature Script. If sunshine appears she escapes to her garden with her Menagerie and notebook.

Nick Jackson – Nick's short fiction has been published in the Amazon bestselling anthologies "Dark Minds" (Bloodhound Books, 2016) and "Twisted's Evil Little Sister" (Create50, 2017), and will next appear in "The Singularity" (Create50, due 2018). He regularly guest blogs about book adaptations, and is working on his first feature script. He lives in Leeds, northern England, on a street controlled by cats.

Fiona Leitch – Screenwriter and novelist Fiona Leitch currently lives on the sunny South Coast of England, where she enjoys scaring her cats by trying out dialogue on them and writing funny, flawed but awesome female characters. Her debut novel 'Dead in Venice' has been shortlisted for the 2018 Audible New Writing Grant, while her screenplays have made the finals of New York's Athena IRIS

Screenwriting Lab 2017 and been shortlisted for the BBC Writers Room. Her short story 'Twisted' has also been selected for the Twisted 50 Volume 2 horror anthology.

Written by Saranne Bensusan

Thank you for taking the time to read the first Anthropocene Chronicles publication! We all hope you enjoyed the read.

The Anthropocene Chronicles isn't just a one off, but rather a franchise of stories told in different ways. On the following pages, you will find the shooting script for the short film 'Lavender's Blue', and the first 10 pages of the spec script of our feature film 'Dissonance'.

'Lavender's Blue' is a short film we made in January of 2018 starring Stine Olsen as Emilie and Natalie Sloth Richter as the voice of Gina. This film is a home video that Emilie made a few days before her 'off day', where she talks about the disappearance of her sister and baby nephew years ago, her suspicions about Gina hiding information from her, and the discovery of an old children's lullaby that had been re-written and used as an underground song of rebellion against the system. We filmed this short in Danish for diversity purposes, and to show that other languages survive in dystopian futures. The following script however is in English.

'Dissonance' is a feature film currently in development and is set 30 years after the end of this book. This film will be in English with some Danish. We catch up with Dominic 30 years after his story in 'The Anthropocene Chronicles', who is still working for LifeStories; and Dotty, who has childhood memories of her grandfather John being dragged away for retirement on his birthday. She lives off grid and leads the 'Outsiders' rebel group. Dominic has a close ally in Beech, who is senior Civil Compliance, and Frank, who is the love of his life.

Maud is still running things with the A.I., however she has more influence over decision making and has now corrupted the A.I. with her ideas through interfacing with it. Citizens assume new laws are coming from the A.I. and trust them, but are now coming from Maud and her desire for ruling power.

Maud plans to infect Citizens to make them more subservient, and Dominic leads a band of rebels from inside to disrupt the A.I. long enough for people to break free. Dominic and Dotty join forces in the fray and end the A.I.

dominance over society, emancipating every human being from their underground lives.

We have scoped out a follow-on TV series where people adjust to their new lives without the comfort of infrastructure, and where they fight among themselves for survival. We also find out that Maud's plan to infect people succeeded and that the A.I. isn't really dead!

The last plans we have are to build more stories like those in this book and produce graphic novels to fill the 30-year gap.

Written by Saranne Bensusan and Rachael Howard

SCENE 1

INT. NIGHT - EMILIE'S APARTMENT POD

Emilie talking to a secret camera. Looking worried, and tired. She whispers into the camera.

EMILIE

Ok. It is 11.53pm on Saturday 15th March 2160. I'm recording this as I think there is something wrong with Gina.

GINA

I'm sorry. I can't hear you. Please speak louder so that I can process your request.

Emilie looks in the direction of her AI unit, but ignores her. We can't see Gina. Emilie looks back at the camera.

EMILIE

For those of you that don't know, Gina is my AI unit.

Emilie looks in the direction of Gina again, and back at the camera. Gina is silent, as if she is listening. Emilie speaks, but quieter.

EMILIE (CONT'D)

When I came in from work this evening, I found Gina was switched off. These units are not supposed to switch off. She started 'malfunctioning' when I asked her about what happened to my sister.

At this point, Emilie holds up a photo frame showing another woman holding a baby.
Gradually talking louder, with an emphasis on the word 'Gina'

EMILIE (CONT'D)

She found out she was pregnant but she wasn't approved for that!
But she had him anyway. And then they both disappeared. I don't know where they went. I tried asking Gina but I didn't get very far....

GINA

Would you like me to perform a new search?

Emilie turns around to address Gina

EMILIE

No thank you

Emilie turns back to the camera and goes back to whispering.

EMILIE (CONT'D)

So I accessed the system at work manually. I discovered there were boarding schools and orphanages for children, and that lots of children are taken away from people like us - even after approval.

There are no records of my sister and I have no idea what my nephew was called. I guess I'll never see them again.

Emilie is emotional and takes a few moments to recompose herself.

EMILIE (CONT'D)

I think Gina knows what I've been trying to research. I think something happened to my sister and nephew. I think that is why she has been 'playing up'. I'm not supposed to know.

Emilie pauses as if to digest this new thought.

EMILIE (CONT'D)

I did find a strange children's lullaby though. I'm not sure
what it has to do with my sister's disappearance, but it must
be important....

Emilie pushes a button and plays a pre-recorded song she
found. She looks at the camera whilst the song is playing:

RECORDING

Lavender's blue, dilly dilly, lavender's green,

When I am king, dilly dilly, you shall be queen,

How will that be, dilly dilly, how will that be?

Because we are strong, dilly dilly, fighters are we.

Keep your voice low, dilly dilly, don't let them hear;

United we'll turn, dilly dilly, nothing to fear.

Up we will rise, dilly dilly, when all can see,

What we've endured, dilly dilly, then we'll be free.

If you should die, dilly dilly, deep in the fray,

You're name shall ring on, dilly dilly, every free day;

When shall it start, dilly dilly, when shall it start?

You'll know the time, dilly dilly, deep in your heart.

At that moment Gina cuts short the dialogue and turns off the music.

GINA

I'm sorry, this song isn't in the database and therefore is not approved by The State.

Emilie rebels.

EMILIE

Lavender's Blue dilly dilly......

At that point, all of the lights go off. Gina has switched all of the electronic devices off and has gone silent. Emilie is just lit from the independent device she is recording on.

CUT TO:

TV SNOW , CIVIL COMPLIANCE LOGO, CREDITS

You can watch the film on your mobile phone for free here:

https://player.vimeo.com/video/262872458

INT. INTERVIEW ROOM - TIME UNDEFINED

DOMINIC, early 60's with grey hair and a few days worth of stubble. He has a pair of glasses on, which is rare as nobody wears glasses these days.

He is sitting in a small windowless room at a small square table. There is an empty chair opposite him and a box of tissues on the table. There is a fluorescent tube light overhead that keeps buzzing intermittently.

There is a case file on the table. It lies open on the medical page with the name Jack Allerton on it. 'Parkinson's Disease' is underlined.

He turns to the next page and sees stamped across it "Referral to The Final Chapter for termination."

Dominic sets up his video imaging device to record the interview just as there is a knock on the door.

DOMINIC

Come in!

JACK ALLERTON, 85 in a once-white boilersuit, shuffles in. His name is on the overall but it is faded.

A guard reaches in and closes the door. They are alone. Dominic takes Jack's hand and shakes it, feels the tremble in the man's arm.

DOMINIC (CONT'D)

Welcome! You must be Jack? Please sit down.

Dominic points to the empty chair in front of the table. Jack nods and shuffles over and cautiously sits down. Dominic pushes the record button and notices Jack's puzzled stare.

DOMINIC (CONT'D)

I'm Dominic Goodwill, the Editor in Chief at LifeStories.

A white uniformed orderly barges in with a tea trolley. They both jump. He hurriedly pours two cups of tea and sploshes it on the table before barging back out. Again a guard reaches in to close the door.

Dominic passes Jack a cup and helps him grip it.

DOMINIC (CONT'D)

I see that you have just had your birthday!

Jack replies, cagey and reserved.

JACK

Yes. My 85th. I'm glad the retirement age is older now. At least my wife didn't get to see this. Arrested me they did on my birthday.

DOMINIC

You know what this is then?

JACK

Yep. Word gets about. We all know what happens to old people. I tell you about my life and you record it on that thing ....

Jack points to the imaging device

JACK (CONT'D)

...and after then I get turned into fertiliser, or mulched or
whatever.

Dominic looks uncomfortable and tidies the already tidy
case file.

DOMINIC

Not quite! This is an opportunity for you to tell us about
your life for the archives for future generations to learn from.
And there is no turning anyone into fertiliser!

Dominic smiles but it doesn't quite reach his eyes.

DOMINIC (CONT'D)

It is more about establishing if you have skills that can be
put to good use whilst you are in this retirement facility.
What did you do before you reached retirement age?

JACK

You mean before you fascists arrested me and detained me

here against my will? Look in your file.

DOMINIC

For the recorder?

Dominic nods his head toward the camera.

JACK

I was a reconditioner. Ya know. One of those folks what go

around to clear the apartments of people what had died..... or

retired.

Jack stares down Dominic. His body may be weak but his

fighting spirit is still there.

JACK (CONT'D)

I clean the flat for new folks to move in. I recondition

apartments. There's some really interesting stuff.

DOMINIC

Like what?

JACK

I remember one woman from years ago. Foreign. Didn't have much. Just a photo of a mother and baby and a video image cube. I found it stuffed down the back of the mattress. Small, easy to slip in my pocket.

Jack winks and Dominic grins.

DOMINIC

You kept it?

JACK

Well, they'd only smash it up. I'm preserving memories. Just like you, aren't I?

Dominic sip his tea and grimaces. He hates what they call tea here. Jack enjoys Dominic's discomfort.

JACK (CONT'D)

Not the posh stuff you're used to is it? What are you?

Second, First Class? That's all us Fourth Classers ever get
down here

DOMINIC

So. Have you still got many the things that you 'preserved'?

JACK

Yep. Loadsa stuff.

Jack folds his arms, enjoying having an audience.

DOMINIC

Like what?

JACK

Photographs. Some dried pressed flowers. Not seen real
flowers before. Clothes from when you could wear what you
like..... I see *you* get to wear what you like.

There is an ugly pause in conversation. Jack enjoys catching
Dominic off guard.

JACK (CONT'D)

That video I mentioned. I took it cos I was curious about
what was on it. Got it home but had nothing to play it on.
Shame that.

DOMINIC

So you binned it?

JACK

Course not. But you never know when stuff gains usefulness.

DOMINIC

Do you have any family?

JACK

Nah. Me n the missus was never approved for that. We
applied o'course but we were declined. We were told we
were lucky to have been given permission to marry. They
started sterilising women after that. Not even asking
permission. My missus went in for a routine check up but
came out with scars on her belly. Prob' cos of the women
just getting pregnant without approval. Criminal.

Dominic offers a tissue when he spots Jack's tears. Sees the hands shake and puts it in his hand for him. He glances at the timer on the recording device. Dominic changes the subject.

DOMINIC

Do you remember The Change?

JACK

Nah. I was born after. My folks remembered it though. Me mam told me that people used to live above ground and that we all had to move underground to be safe from radiation. I see that posh lady's broadcasts. She's not like you lot. She looks after us she does. She says we still can't live above ground yet, but she is working on it. I like her. What's her name?

DOMINIC

Maud. Maud Delancy.

JACK

Yeah Maud. Good woman.

Dominic forces a smile.

DOMINIC

I think we are done here. You are free to go back to your room. Guard!

He helps Jack to his feet and the guard takes over to lead the shuffling man away. Jack doesn't even look back.

Dominic ticks the box on the file next to the word "Interviewed" and extracts the recording cartridge, a small 2cm squared metal cube from the camera.

INT. OUTSIDE JACK'S APARTMENT ROOM, LOWER LEVELS - TIME UNKNOWN

Dominic checks all is clear before pulling out an electronic hacking device and puts it up to the door plate of Jack's apartment room. It clicks open with ease.

INT. JACK'S APARTMENT ROOM, LOWER LEVELS - TIME UNKNOWN

The room light pops on automatically as he walks in showing the sheer scale of junk that Jack had collected. A single room with every surface smothered in a jumble of small artifacts. Just half the bed remains for Jack to sleep in.

A large collection of dust covered ornaments littered the one shelf that was in the room, and boxes upon boxes of people's possessions were stocked up from floor to near-ceiling height.

Dominic pulled down the first box. In it he finds old dusty photo albums, a child's swimsuit that was falling apart, and a couple of books.

Dominic looks at the faded photos. People going on holiday, having fun at the park, pictures at Christmas. Dominic hears a noise in the corridor and closed the album quickly.

By the time Dominic got to the fourth box, he hits gold. He finds several video cubes in a case and pockets the lot. He also found a tube of suncream.

He examines it. What was different about this was that whilst everything else was old this was new and was made last month.

DOMINIC

Why would anyone be making this?

He suddenly hears voices in the corridor outside close by and quickly pockets the suncream. He heads to the door where he listens.

INT. OUTSIDE JACK'S APARTMENT ROOM, LOWER LEVELS - TIME UNKNOWN

A team of three reconditioners are heading towards Jack's apartment. They are all wearing the same white boiler suits. A Chinese woman, BEECH, mid-40's, wearing a senior level Civil Compliance police uniform steps out of a stairwell and intercepts the group.

BEECH

Would you mind coming this way gentlemen?

Beech points to the stairwell.

The three men look scared.

BEECH (CONT'D)

Don't worry, it is just a routine inspection. It won't take five
minutes.

The men file out into the stairwell.

INT. JACK'S APARTMENT ROOM, LOWER LEVELS - TIME UNKNOWN

Dominic listens to Beech's voice and uses this as a time to
escape. He has one last look around the room before leaving.

INT. DOMINIC'S APARTMENT - TIME UNKNOWN

The door slides open as Dominic removes his hand from the
ID plate. The apartment wakes up as he enters and the door
closes behind him.

It is much more luxurious than Jack's. He has several rooms
rather than just the one and a wall that has an electronic
display of a woodland forest looking real. A few moments

later there is a knock at the door. Dominic opens it. It is
Beech. Dominic lets her in.

DOMINIC

Thanks for earlier!

BEECH

No problem. You were in there a bloody long time. Did you
get the video?

DOMINIC

I'm just about to find out.

Dominic sits at the docking station and works through the
cubes. The first two are damaged. Just static. The third is a
video of a woman wearing a white boiler suit speaking
another language. The name on the boiler suit is Emilie.

EMILIE (O.S)

Okay. Klokken er 11.53, og det er lørdag d.15. Marts 2160.
Jeg Optager dette fordi jeg tror der er noget galt med Gina

Beech starts talking over the video.

BEECH

It's in Danish!

DOMINIC

Shhh! I want to know what she says

At this point, Emilie holds up a photo frame showing another woman holding a baby.

EMILIE (O.S)

Hun fandt ud af at hun var gravid,

men hun var ikke godkendt til det!

Men hun fødte ham alligevel. Og så

forsvandt de begge. Jeg ved ikke,

hvor de tog hen. Jeg forsøgte at

spørge Gina, men jeg kom ikke særligt langt ....

DOMINIC (CONT'D)

That is what Jack was talking about. How some women just

got themselves pregnant without getting permission.

BEECH

My mother was a child born without permission. She was

eventually taken away and put in a home.

They continue to watch the video for a few more minutes.

EMILIE

Jeg fandt dog en mærkelig

vuggevise. Jeg er ikke sikker på,

hvad det har at gøre med min

søsters forsvinden, men det må være

vigtigt ....

In the video Emilie pushes a button and a song plays.

RECORDING

Lavender's blue, dilly dilly,

lavender's green,

When I am king, dilly dilly, you

shall be queen,How will that be, dilly dilly, how will that be?

Because we are strong, dilly dilly,

fighters are we.

Keep your voice low, dilly dilly,

don't let them hear;

United we'll turn, dilly dilly,

nothing to fear.

Up we will rise, dilly dilly, when

all can see,

What we've endured, dilly dilly,

then we'll be free.

If you should die, dilly dilly,

deep in the fray,

You're name shall ring on, dilly

dilly, every free day;

When shall it start, dilly dilly,

when shall it start?

You'll know the time, dilly dilly,

deep in your heart.

The music cuts off and Gina says that the song is not allowed. At that point Emilie starts singing the song on her own. The video ends before she gets to the end of the first line.

DOMINIC

For fanden!! Jeg kender denne sang! This is a song of

rebellion!

Dominic searches for a video in his LifeStories digital archive and plays it. It is an interview of an old woman from 30 years ago.

YOUNG DOMINIC (O.S)

Are you Maizy?

MAIZY

Yes? Maizy Goulden

YOUNG DOMINIC (O.S.)

I'm Dominic

BEECH

Oh my god! This is my grandmother! I've never seen her before.

Dominic fast forwards the video.

YOUNG DOMINIC

Were you approved to have a child?

MAIZY

No. I didn't have someone approve me for motherhood. I just did it. Well, my husband and I just did it. She is so beautiful. Can you see those sweet curls at the back of her neck. Smell her head. That Baby Smell, that is. My lovely Flower. That's what I've named her.

Dominic races through the video again.

MAIZY (CONT'D)

If you should die, dilly dilly, deep in the fray, Your name shall ring on, dilly dilly, every free day; When shall it start, dilly dilly, when shall it start? You'll know the time, dilly dilly, deep in your heart.

Dominic stops the video.

DOMINIC

I remember your grandmother made the nurses anxious

when she sang that song.

BEECH

I never knew why it was important. I never met Granny
Maizy as Mum was taken away as a child. Mum used to sing
that song to me when I was small..... We need to get the song
out there. Use it for our campaign. Maybe through video or
something?

Dominic nods his head in agreement.

DOMINIC

Wordsworth, what happened to Emilie?

WORDSWORTH

Why do you want to know that Dominic?

DOMINIC

Just satisfy my curiosity. OK?

WORDSWORTH

She was arrested for Disorderly Conduct and Deficient
Contribution and terminated as per the standard protocol on

Tuesday 18th March 2160

DOMINIC

Thank you, Wordsworth. That will be all.

BEECH

So, just three days after this video was made she was put to death?! So singing this song could get you into the final chapter....

DOMINIC

I don't know of anyone who has sung it and lived to talk about it. Emilie was a Martyr.

Dominic reaches under his mattress and removes a small bottle of 2175 whiskey. It is half empty. He carefully pours two small tumblers before setting Emilie's cube playing again.

To be continued.......